Epitaph of Vengeance

By the same author

Rodeo Renegade

Epitaph of Vengeance

TY KIRWAN

A Black Horse Western

ROBERT HALE · LONDON

© Ty Kirwan 1998
First published in Great Britain 1998

ISBN 0 7090 6238 9

Robert Hale Limited
Clerkenwell House
Clerkenwell Green
London EC1R 0HT

The right of Ty Kirwan
to be identified as author of this work has been
asserted by her in accordance with the Copyright,
Designs and Patents Act 1988.

637209
MORAY COUNCIL
Department of Technical
& Leisure Services
W F

Photoset in North Wales by
Derek Doyle & Associates, Mold, Flintshire.
Printed and bound in Great Britain by
WBC Book Manufacturers Limited, Bridgend.

Prologue

A weariness in the way they sat their ponies said they had ridden a long distance. There were two of them. A brave who rode slightly ahead of a squaw as they approached the public square at Humboldt, Kansas. They came unnoticed by the men of Troop D, 6th Kansas Cavalry, who were eating their noon meal in the comfort of a pleasant spring day in that year of 1863. A sentry anxiously watched the Indians come his way. Young and afraid, he looked beyond the pair as if expecting a war party to come hooting and hollering over the horizon at any moment. Swallowing several times to find his voice, causing his prominent adam's apple to leap violently, he called to the duty sergeant.

Sergeant George Milnar strode up to stand beside the sentry, increasing the lines in his sun-baked face by squinting at the riders. A tough, experienced veteran, Milnar permitted himself an inward smile at the sentry's jumpiness. He drawled, 'I guess we ain't under attack, son. These two are from the Osage Reserve.'

Yet there was something about the nearing Osages that prepared Milnar for bad news. They had a funereal aura as they moved slowly along. Conversely, there was a concealed but detectable urgency to them as they both lithely dismounted in front of the sergeant.

The brave wore his hair close-cropped in the Osage style, with a central ridge called a roach. His dress was typical of the Plains Indian; a skin shirt, buffalo robe, leggings and moccasins. The Indian girl had the haughty beauty of an Apache rather than an Osage. Her long black hair was parted from her forehead to the nape of her neck, with the part line painted red. She had the bearing of a princess, but none of the trappings denoting Osage hierarchy.

'We come to speak with Captain Anello,' she told him in a melodious voice, her English good.

A distant look on the brave's face told Milnar that the Osage hadn't understood a word his female companion had spoken. The young squaw held the sergeant's gaze steadily as he objected. 'It just ain't that easy, miss. This here's the army, and I just can't run and fetch my commanding officer for you nor anyone else.'

'I am Loossantech,' she told Milnar, confident that she need say no more.

Though the name meant nothing to the sergeant, it was common knowledge that the captain had got himself involved with an Osage girl. There were rumours that August Anello was prepared to abandon his career for her if necessary. Should that occur it would be a tragedy, for the captain was regarded as one of the finest, if not the finest, officer in the outfit.

Sergeant Milnar looked his striking visitor over. Wearing a long buckskin dress, knee-high leggings and moccasins, she was truly beautiful, as Captain Anello's squaw was said to be. But either an obtuse memory or instinct, Milnar knew not which, convinced him that this wasn't his commanding officer's woman.

She spoke to him again, not sharply but insistently. 'Please, tell Captain Anello that Loossantech is here.'

'You'll probably cost me my stripes,' Milnar told her resignedly, a little intimidated by her. The Indians had a disturbing directness that insincerity had robbed the white man of. He questioned the sentry. 'Did you get that name, Brierly?'

'Loossantech,' Brierly, having difficulty getting his tongue round the Osage name, broke it up awkwardly into syllables.

'Then go tell Captain Anello that this lady's here,' Milnar ordered. 'And try not to forget her name.'

The squaw turned from the sergeant then to exchange a few abrupt sentences with the brave in their own tongue. Though not an especially sensitive man, Milnar was hurt by a feeling of being dismissed as the beautiful girl switched her attention from him. Her very presence made a man feel somehow special. Worry nagged Milnar. He had a feeling he had done the right thing by sending for the captain, but he'd been around long enough to know that the army often turned the right thing wrong, to the detriment of the soldier innocently making the mistake.

Then he saw Brierly returning in the bent-kneed lope that passed for a walk with him. The boy had the ambition to be a good soldier, but his body let him down. Captain Anello was a little way behind. As immaculately turned-out as usual, fair-haired and handsome, the commanding officer was every inch a soldier. He came up to them, bright blue eyes taking in and assessing the situation. Anello was indelibly marked by the authority that came from years of being in command.

'What is it, Loossantech?' the captain enquired in the deeply resonant voice that could turn even a senior non-commissioned officer's knees to jelly when dealing with a disciplinary matter. 'What brings you here?'

'There has been trouble at the village, Captain Anello,' the Osage girl replied. her dark eyes locked with Anello's blue ones. 'A party of white men came. Our tribesmen fought them, but we have many dead.'

'When was this?' Anello asked sharply. It surprised Sergeant Milnar to see his commanding officer's poise under threat.

'Two days ago, Captain. Tall Bear and Long Rope want you to come.'

Milnar recognized the names as belonging to two young chiefs. Peaceable, sensible fellows, they were efficient warriors who were trusted by their elders and the army. He observed his commanding officer, a man with whom he had served long and knew well. Anello was bracing himself to make an enquiry that plainly meant a lot to him.

'Silver Moon?' August Anello asked.

Seeing the squaw release the captain's gaze and avert her face without answering, Milnar understood. Silver Moon would be the name of August Anello's squaw. The Indian girl's refusal to answer said everything. For a second, a very brief second, there was a slight, uncharacteristic slump to Anello's shoulders. But then he regained his old military style and rapped out orders for the sergeant.

'Have half the troop mount up, Sergeant Milnar,' Captain Anello commanded. 'Give Lieutenant Meadows my compliments and inform him that he will remain here in charge of the remainder of the troop. We will be riding to the village.'

It will be a really long ride, Milnar commented to himself as he hurried away. Having patrolled the vast reserve, which was separated from Missouri's western border by a buffer strip, fifty miles long by twenty-five miles wide, called Cherokee Neutral Land, the sergeant was aware that whole Osage villages were picked up and moved when grazing for horses became poor. Wherever Loossantech's village was, it would be far away. The Osages still travelled annually to the western plains on their buffalo hunts, which meant that the western limit of the reserve was loosely somewhere around the Arkansas River.

With the southern boundary of the reserve being Indian Territory, the Cherokee Nation, there was a vagueness about the land. Though neither the Union nor Confederate forces claimed dominance, the area was made dangerous by probing patrols sent out by both sides; the Union scouts coming out of Humboldt and Fort Scott in Kansas, and the Confederates crossing the border from the Cherokee Nation.

All of this Milnar knew, and it filled him with misgivings. But later he was pleased to discover that though the ride to the Osage village was lengthy and exhausting, it wasn't as long as he had feared it would be.

At midnight came the first indication that they were nearing their destination. The tired troopers shivered as the eerie wailing of Indian women in mourning came to them through the darkness. Riding at the side of Captain Anello, Sergeant Milnar exchanged glances with him. The volume of grief was an indication of the severity of what had occurred here.

Entering the village they were confronted, even at that late hour, by Osage women bowing low, swaying from side to side, dragging their hair through the dirt as they howled and screeched their lamentations. Milnar could see eight dead warriors, all tied to a tree in sitting positions, wearing war paint and dressed in finery.

Leaving the troop mounted, Anello and Milnar got down from their horses. Tall Bear and Long Rope, waiting impassively for them, stood with arms folded across their chests. But Loossantech, who walked at the side of the two army men, steered them without touching either man or signalling in any way, to the right of the two chiefs. When the squaw stopped, concerned eyes on Captain Anello, Milnar saw three children, two boys and a girl, laid out in death on a grassy bank. Although the little bodies had been cleaned up, gruesome injuries were still evident, making it plain that they had died in the attack. Beside them lay the slim body of a young Indian woman, eyes closed, her lovely face peaceful. The sergeant assumed that this was Silver Moon. He covertly watched August Anello stand looking sadly down at the dead girl. For a few moments he was an ordinary man, a grieving man. Then stiffening his back, his lean, good-looking face as inscrutable as those of the Osages around them, he walked with soldierly bearing to where the chiefs stood.

With Loossantech as interpreter, her dark face dramatic in the moonlight, Tall Bear went over the events of two days ago. Six men, all of them drunk and wearing blue tunics, had ridden into the camp. To the Osages they had looked like soldiers from Humboldt, but the Indians were familiar with the faces of the 6th Kansas Cavalry, and they didn't recognize these strangers. Heavily armed, the raiders had suddenly turned violent, killing eight braves and three children before everyone except Silver Moon had scattered to safety among the trees. The Indian girl had been captured, and though he was sure Loossantech had thoughtfully toned down the interpretation of what had happened to Silver Moon, hearing it sickened Milnar. He felt an immense sympathy for his commanding officer, and admired the stoical way in which he reacted to the ghastly story.

'Does either Tall Bear or Long Rope know who these men are?' Anello asked tersely.

Shaking her head, Loossantech lowered her voice to say confidentially, 'There is something else, Captain Anello, but my chiefs are afraid they will be punished if they tell you.'

'They weren't responsible for this,' the captain used a sweep of his hand to indicate the dead bodies, 'so they have nothing to fear. Tell them that, Loossantech.'

The Indian girl hesitated. Anello said brusquely, 'Tell them what I said. Don't you want those killers caught?'

For the first time since she had arrived in Humboldt, Loossantech dropped the cool control that came naturally to an Indian. Rounding on Anello, eyes blazing and her top lip lifting from white teeth in a snarl, she angrily hissed, 'You forget, Captain, that Silver Moon was my sister!'

'I'm sorry,' Anello murmured, and Milnar saw him reach out a hand to the girl's shoulder. The captain cancelled the movement before he actually touched Loossantech.

Calming, the Indian girl said something in the Osage language to the two chiefs. Neither of them were reassured by Captain Anello's promise that they wouldn't be punished, and both were fearful. Tall

Bear remained quiet, but Long Rope said something to Loossantech that had her turn to Anello.

'They killed one of the men, Captain Anello.'

'Where is the body?' Anello was asking, but the first rays of a dawn sun were pushing the night away, and Milnar nudged his captain, gesturing with his head to where vultures circled.

'I reckon that answers your question, sir,' the sergeant said.

'I guess we'd better take a look, Sergeant Milnar,' the captain said, face grim as they looked up at the huge, ugly, wheeling black birds.

None of the Indians, not even Loossantech, followed the two soldiers as they walked away. Some fifty yards from the village, lying on bloodstained sand, was a body so horribly mutilated that it was barely recognizable as the remains of a man. The clothing had been ripped to shreds so that it was unidentifiable. Heat over two days had caused the flesh to decompose fast. The foul reek had the captain and the sergeant covering their mouths and noses with a gloved hand.

'Arrange a burial detail, Sergeant Milnar,' Anello ordered, adding, because of the awful stench, 'Make sure the men tie cloths containing asafoetida over their faces.'

Both chiefs looked apprehensive as August Anello came back from having viewed the sliced-up body. Able to understand their wrath because he felt a cold but terrible anger himself over the death of Silver Moon, the captain couldn't, never had and never would, accept the savagery with which the Indians exacted revenge.

Standing waiting in the shadows, Loossantech had taken on a neutrality. Making no attempt to approach Anello, neither was she backing away from him.

Deep in thought, the captain was silent as he tried to grasp an elusive point. Then it came to him. Having killed the Confederate officer, the Osages would have gone through his pockets before mutilating the corpse. He needed to know what they had found, but was aware that cunning would be required. Apart from fear that he would punish them for robbing the body of a white man, the Osages were covetous, and would not easily part with what they now considered to be their property.

Anello walked slowly to Loossantech. 'Tall Bear and Long Rope are keeping something from me. Am I right?'

'I believe so, but I cannot be sure,' the Indian girl replied uncomfortably.

She began a conversation with the two chiefs that was highly animated by Indian standards. Long Rope started to walk away, an annoyed expression on his face, and when Tall Bear showed signs of going with him, the harshness of Anello's tone to Loossantech had both the male Indians delay leaving.

'Tell them, Loossantech,' the captain said, 'that I know they have robbed the white man.'

Not knowing what the officer had said, the chiefs were aware that it was important. They looked to

Epitaph of Vengeance 15

Loossantech for the interpretation. Both of them said something angrily when the girl had finished speaking.

'They say that they took nothing from the soldier-coat, Captain,' Loossantech reported.

Not prepared to be thwarted, August Anello was ready to renege on the promise he had made earlier not to punish the Osages. 'If they refuse to give me what they took from the dead man, then I will arrest them both and take them back to Humboldt and have them hanged for this killing.'

When Loossantech told the chiefs what the captain had said, it sparked off another, even more prolonged, discussion in the Osage language. At last, an unhappy-looking Tall Bear walked away to return holding some documents which, with abject reluctance, he handed to the Indian girl. In turn, Loossantech passed them to Anello.

Water-stained, bloody and torn, the papers revealed that the killers had all been commissioned officers in the Confederate Army. Their official mission had been to determine the strength of the Union forces at Humboldt, and to make contact with any Confederate sympathizers. Alcohol had caused that mission to go disastrously wrong.

With Sergeant Milnar looking over his shoulder, Captain Anello silently read the names: Captain Edward G. Witsell, lieutenants Gardiner Woodward, John S. Peck, George L. Mallory, Alexander Mack, Antony Siegle.

'I wonder which of them the men are burying, sir?' Milnar mused.

'It makes little difference, Sergeant Milnar,' Anello grimly replied. 'He has gone a little earlier than the rest of them, that's all.'

Milnar walked away then as Loossantech came quietly up to his commanding officer. Before he was out of earshot, the sergeant felt the guilt of an eavesdropper as he overheard the Indian girl say, 'I know that you will get vengeance for us. When the sun goes down this night, Captain Anello, think of me. I will be standing high on a hill asking the Great Spirit to take good care of my sister and the dead children and braves, and I will also ask that you be brought back safely to us . . . to me.'

The emphasis the Indian girl had put on her last two words, *to me*, required no explanation. Never having been a ladies' man, Sergeant Milnar nevertheless felt a stab of envy as he stood awaiting orders in the crisp air of a spring morning. It was neither a deep nor vindictive jealousy that assailed him. There was nothing that would induce him to feel animosity toward his commanding officer. Rather it was a personal regret that fate hadn't seen fit to give him the looks and charm that August Anello had been blessed with. Milnar had seen officers with similar feelings toward Captain Anello, but in them it had caused bitter resentment.

Recovering swiftly, the sergeant came to attention as a thoughtful captain came up to him. 'Your orders, sir?'

The burial detail was returning, a sick-looking Private Brierly among them. The sight of him reminded Milnar that there was a lot more to soldiering out here than firing a gun. As a private, the sergeant had helped bury hundreds of Indians who had died from typhoid. He and the other soldiers had worn masks, *bandanas* soaked in a strong-smelling resin, but thirty-four of his comrades had later succumbed to the disease. Beset by death throughout his adult life, George Milnar had never been able to adjust to it.

He found it strange that the howls of the mourning women, so distressing when they arrived, were continuing without any of the soldiers now noticing. What he took to be the whole of the village had assembled now. Lined up in uneven ranks, they stood silently surveying the soldiers as they prepared to leave.

It was ironic, Milnar thought, that they had come out in force to take care of whoever had attacked the Osage village, but now they could do nothing. A skirmish between Captain Anello's men and a Confederate patrol would be fairly commonplace and acceptable to the military commanders at Fort Scott. For half of Troop D to go in pursuit of the remaining five killers would be suicidal should they run into a Confederate force of any real size. Frustrating though it was for Captain Anello, he would know that to mount a pursuit expedition from here would result either in the death of all of them, or a court martial for him.

'Are the men up to riding back to Humboldt, Sergeant?'

'In my opinion, sir, both the men and the horses are in need of rest.'

'Right, Sergeant Milnar,' Anello gave an emphatic nod as if this was the conclusion he, too, had reached. 'Rest them close by until noon, then mount them up and get back to town.'

Seeing his commanding officer swing up into the saddle, Milnar enquired, 'Aren't you staying with us, sir?'

'No. I'm riding to Fort Scott for permission to take a detail in pursuit of the men who did this,' Anello answered. 'I take it that you'd like to go after them with me, Sergeant?'

'Indeed, sir,' Sergeant Milnar came to stand close to the head of the captain's horse, the years they had spent together permitting him enough licence to continue. 'With all due respect to the dead Osages, sir, I can't see permission being granted, even if the offenders had been Union soldiers.'

His sergeant was speaking the truth, August Anello knew that but didn't want to accept it. Reining his horse round, ready to ride out, he spoke while moving off. 'With or without permission, George, I swear that I will hunt those men down!'

One

'Apart from inviting you to share our simple meal, stranger, I can offer you nought but our blessing.'

The nun was young. The restricting wimple could not conceal her prettiness. Walking away from five other sisters who were working on the conversion of semi-derelict buildings, she had come bravely, because there seemed to be no men on the tiny settlement, to meet Anello when he rode up. Despite the almost challenging stance of her slender frame, Anello could detect a growing fear far back in her eyes. Wanting to put her at ease, Anello dismounted swiftly, pulling off his stetson and slapping it against his leg to knock off the dust as he replied.

'I'll gladly accept both the meal and the blessing, Sister,' Anello said. 'But I'll pay for the food.'

'Both things I offered come free,' she said assuringly, managing to give a weak smile as she assessed him as no threat. 'But if you feel like making a small donation to our cause, then I won't try to stop you. I am Sister Joseph.'

'August Anello, Sister Joseph,' he introduced himself. It required effort not to prefix his name with 'Captain'. At ease in any company, even with those of high rank, he became awkward now. Uncertain whether it was right to shake the hand of a nun, he went part-way through the motion, with her responding similarly. Neither of them completed the gesture, and they shared short laughs of embarrassment.

The nun was a little flustered as he walked at her side toward the only completed building. Regaining her cool composure before they reached the wooden shack, Sister Joseph explained, 'This is our dormitory. We eat and sleep in there, and we managed to squeeze a little classroom in at the end of the building. These,' she gestured to a row of barns that the other nuns were busily working on, 'will eventually be cabins to house orphaned Cherokee children.'

'You are doing a great job here, Sister Joseph,' Anello complimented her, frowning before he continued, 'but, with respect, this isn't women's work.'

'You're right,' she agreed, her habit making a gentle swishing sound as she walked. 'This is God's work, Mr Anello.'

'But are there no men to help you?'

Stopping outside the door of the dormitory, she studied him for a few moments. An aroma of heated pork grease reached Anello to screw his empty stomach into a painful knot. No food had passed his lips for three days and nights, a period in which he had snatched only a few hours' sleep in short stretches.

Epitaph of Vengeance 21

'You look very tired and hungry, Mr Anello,' the nun said concernedly. 'I will tell you about the mission later. You may wash up at a water butt at the rear of the dormitory, and by that time Sister Miriam should have the food prepared.'

'Thank you,' Anello said, and was about to turn away when Sister Joseph spoke firmly to him.

'Mr Anello. While accepting that the gun and bullet-belt you wear are your property, it is offensive to me, as I am sure it would be to the other sisters. Might I keep it out of harm's way while you are our guest?'

Hesitating, Anello ran through the possible dangers that might come from him being unarmed. There seemed no threat to him in this isolated place, so he unbuckled his gunbelt, wrapped it around the holstered, standard-issue Colt, and handed the bundle to her.

Over-balancing slightly under the unexpected weight, the nun recovered and thanked him with the Latin for 'God be with you' – *Dominus vobiscum*.

'*Et cum spiritu tuo*.' Anello automatically responded with 'And with your spirit'.

'You are of the faith, Mr Anello!' she exclaimed, looking pleased.

'A very long time ago, Sister Joseph,' he said apologetically, feeling gauche, which was out of character for him.

'Time is not important,' the pretty nun wagged a finger at him. 'Now, go wash up, the food will be on the table. A hungry man is an abomination.'

At the water barrel, Anello stripped off his shirt. Scooping water out with both hands cupped, he splashed it over himself, enjoying the stimulating tingle as his tiredness was washed away.

He had pushed himself and his horse hard since leaving Fort Scott, passing through dangerous country. As Sergeant Milnar had predicted, his request had been rejected out of hand at the fort. Until Colonel Blueth had put it into perspective, Anello, normally a man who thought on a wide front, had seen the slaying of Silver Moon and the other Osages only in a personal, very narrow way.

'Captain Anello,' the colonel had addressed him sternly. 'You are asking permission to go after five grayback officers. Damn it, Captain, we are at war with the whole Confederate army. You want to be allowed to ride to the Cherokee Nation like some kind of sheriff leading a posse. That is enemy territory, Captain, and I cannot officially comply with what you ask of me.'

Blueth's use of the word 'officially' had encouraged Anello to take a chance. He told the colonel, 'This is important to me, sir. If necessary I will resign my commission and leave the army.'

'I understand what it means to you, Captain Anello,' Blueth had replied in a quiet voice. 'Because I have always respected you as both an officer and a man, and in the knowledge that I can depend on your judgment, I am prepared to allow you indefinite leave of absence. You can return to the army, at your present rank, at the time of your choice. But I must warn that your absence in a time of war, although sanctioned, will reflect poorly on your military record.'

Appreciating the colonel's concern for him, Anello had already accepted that, should he survive the vengeance trail he was going on, his army career would be devoid of the promise it had previously held.

Entering the dormitory, he found Sister Joseph smiling a welcome for him from where she sat at the head of a crude, wooden table. Another nun, as silent as a ghost, led him to the far end, where he sat and bowed his head with the nuns as Sister Joseph said grace. The meal was a frugal one: pancakes made from flour, water and salt fried in pork grease. In addition there were some dry, unappetizing crusts.

'Perhaps you would later like to see what we are attempting here, Mr Anello,' she said as they ate. 'You commented on the fact that there are no men here. That is due to the Church being unwilling, or more likely unable, to support what was regarded as my wild scheme for this place. I am quietly confident that when the sisters and myself have finished our work, priests will be sent here and we will rapidly expand. I think if you call on us again in a year or two, the size and strength of our mission will amaze you.'

A year or two? The outcome of the conflict between North and South was still very much in doubt, and Anello, about to take up a position between the two warring factions, couldn't afford to look that far ahead. His future extended no further than ensuring his beloved Silver Moon slept in peace by avenging her.

The meal, such as it was. ended. Anello found his hunger appeased more by a sensation of nausea than by satisfaction. Sister Joseph was studying him covertly but intently.

'Our need for penance here, Mr Anello,' she said, in what seemed an attempt at excusing the meal, 'is much reduced by the poor quality of the food available to us.'

'I enjoyed the meal, Sister Joseph,' he told her gallantly.

The nun laughed, a sound that held a parallel prettiness to her face. 'I judge that we can't regard your lie as a mortal sin, Mr Anello, because you told it for such good reasons.'

'I am no longer hungry, Sister Joseph,' he said truthfully in support of his earlier untruth, standing, ready to leave but not really wanting to go.

'If only your other malady could be cured so easily, Mr Anello,' Sister Joseph said wistfully as she, too, stood from the table.

They walked out of the door together into air pleasantly cooled by evening. Shadows cast by the mesquite were lengthening. In the middle distance, here and there on rocky ridges or hummocks, giant cacti pointed bare green fingers accusingly at the sky.

'You believe that something ails me, Sister Joseph?' a curious Anello questioned.

Looking to where a lowering sun was purpling the

sky, the nun didn't really answer, but quoted from the Bible: ' "Be not hasty in thy spirit to be angry; for anger resteth in the bosom of fools." '

'That's the nicest way I've ever been called a fool,' Anello said, smiling at the nun, inwardly perturbed at how accurately she had read him.

'Forgive me,' she said, her manner changing, becoming less serious. 'Now, Mr Anello, you are a weary traveller and our hospitality will stretch to giving you rest. Come, I will have Sister Philomena fetch blankets and you can spend this night in the classroom. In the morning, before you take your leave of us, I will take you on a tour of my modest holy empire. If, of course, that would be of interest to you.'

'I look forward to that,' he assured her.

Anello was then so tired that he gratefully took the blankets and went into the classroom. It had been difficult for him to take his leave of the nun. Her presence relaxed him while, inexplicably, at the same time affected him in a way that her holy orders should have prohibited. When he lay on the wooden floor he was overtaken by exhaustion. Sleeping long and late, it was Sister Joseph's voice that awakened him.

The sun was already high as he went to the glassless window to look out. What he saw made him jerk his head back out of sight. Sister Joseph, head high in the way she had met him, was facing three ruffians. All of the men were unwashed and unshaven: saddletramps of the worst kind. Two were white, while the third was a massive, coal-black, brutal-looking negro wearing a tattered blue uniform of the Union army. Anello guessed that this was a former slave who, protected as a soldier by the Union government and known as a contraband, had escaped.

Anello heard Sister Joseph say, 'All of you are welcome to our food and our blessing.'

The man in the middle, a cross-eyed fellow with scars across his temple to testify that at some time an attempt had been made to scalp him alive, leaned on his rifle, leering at Sister Joseph.

'Now that's mighty hospitable of you, lady, but it's like this here,' the man said. 'Me'n the boys been on the trail a tolerable long time, and we'm looking for entertainment that's a heap more interesting than some gospel meeting.'

'Sure am,' the big negro agreed with his companion, a white-toothed grin beaming across his black face. As he spoke, he reached out a big hand, the fingers clutching Sister Joseph's habit. Even at the distance Anello was from the grim scene, he heard the material tear as the young nun pulled away in horror.

An incensed elderly nun ran up to protect Sister Joseph, putting herself between the young nun and the three men. Laughing at her, the man in the middle lifted the stock of his rifle just an inch or so from the ground. Holding the muzzle with both hands he gave the weapon a little swing. The stock smacked against the elderly nun's ankle with a crack that said a bone had been broken. Yet the old

Epitaph of Vengeance 27

woman, staggering sideways, uttered not one cry to register the intense pain her ankle had to be causing her. But she did cry out loud in protest when the negro leapt at Sister Joseph, holding her to him in a bear hug.

A seething Anello had to force himself to remain in the classroom. The window was too small for him to get through. The front door was the only exit. But he was unarmed, and any of the three men could gun him down before he had the chance to help Sister Joseph.

It was then that he spotted Sister Philomena, the nun who had fetched him blankets the previous night. Her plain face full of terror, she was skulking behind one of the incomplete cabins. Clinging to a half-finished wall she peered over it at the grim drama being played out. The nun was within whispering range of Anello.

'Sister Philomena!' he hissed guardedly.

Startled by hearing her name called, she looked in every direction other than at Anello. Then she looked his way and he called again, beckoning her over. She came to the window to look questioningly up at him. Head on one side like an alert but nervous bird, she waited to hear what he had to say.

'Sister Joseph has my gun,' Anello said, and when she nodded to confirm that she knew this, he asked urgently, 'Do you know where it is?'

'In the tool shed,' she replied, 'hidden away.'

'Can you get it for me without those men seeing you?'

Sister Philomena gave this question serious thought, frustrating Anello as he heard a harrowing scream come from Sister Joseph at the front of the building. It was accompanied by inane laughter from the men. The elderly nun with the injured ankle knelt on the ground in prayer. Anello knew that she was beseeching the Lord's help for Sister Joseph.

'I could get it,' Sister Philomena told him apprehensively. 'But Sister Joseph would not want me to touch a gun.'

'I'm sure that she will forgive you on this occasion,' Anello told her urgently.

The nun went off then, furtively but at some speed. Returning, lugging the heavy Colt and gunbelt in both arms, she passed it through the window to him. Poised to run off, wanting nothing of what was about to happen, she paused when he called to her.

'Sister Philomena! I need more help from you.'

Her whole body trembling now, the nun's bottom lip quivered as she told Anello, 'I am too frightened to be of use to you.'

'You can do it for Sister Joseph,' Anello used a tone that he hoped would calm her. 'You see that stone down by your right foot? All I want you to do is pick it up.'

Bending to do as he said, the nun straightened up, the stone in her right hand and bewilderment on her face. 'Yes?'

'When I tell you, Sister Philomena, start steadily counting to ten. When you reach ten, throw the stone at that tin bath-tub over there. Can you do that?'

'I don't understand how that will help Sister Joseph!' the nun said, confused and filled with doubt.

'It will, trust me,' Anello spoke as he buckled on his gunbelt. 'Please, do as I say, Sister Philomena. Start counting now!'

With no option but to rely on the nun carrying out what he asked, Anello went out of the classroom and through the dormitory toward the front door, counting inside his head all the time. He felt pretty sure that Sister Philomena would throw the stone. The possible big problem would come from her rate of counting varying widely from his.

Nine! He reached the door, hand on the latch. With ten coming up in his mind, Colt in his right hand, he pulled the door open wide and stepped out, just as Sister Philomena's stone boomingly hit the bath-tub.

The heads of all three men had turned to where the noise had come from. A dishevelled Sister Joseph was being held securely in the thick, powerful arms of the negro. With a clear space between the two white men and himself, Anello opened fire. Selecting bodies because they made larger targets than heads, he put a bullet through the heart of the man nearest to him. The scar-faced man still leaned on his rifle, and Anello's second shot came so fast that it took the man by surprise. But Anello's bullet was deflected by striking the barrel of the man's rifle. Instead of entering the body cleanly, the flattened bullet tore away part of the scar-faced man's left side, exposing flesh and entrails.

Letting his rifle fall, the man, face distorted by agony, put both hands to his side in a futile attempt at pressing his bloody innards back in. Twisting this way and that, the man fell backwards over his fallen companion, crashing to the ground. Although mortally wounded, instinct had the man struggle up onto all fours until another bullet from Anello went in under the chin of his raised head, mercifully putting him out of his misery.

Holding Sister Joseph as a shield, the black man had stooped to pick up a length of timber, which he threw at Anello. Bringing his gun round after killing the scar-faced man, hoping for a shot at the negro without endangering the nun, Anello saw the heavy piece of wood coming at him, but had no time to avoid it.

Thudding against his right temple, it knocked Anello off his feet. Hitting the ground, he didn't lose consciousness, but his brain spun blackly for half a minute.

When the darkness inside his head cleared, Anello found himself lying on his back in the dust. His Colt also lay on the ground, several yards from him. The huge black man had come over to stand towering above him. Bending down, the negro grasped Anello's right shoulder with one hand, his strong fingers digging in while he gripped Anello's right thigh with the other hand.

Epitaph of Vengeance 31

Effortlessly, the powerful black man lifted Anello up from the ground. Taking a deep breath, the negro then raised Anello so that he held him at arm's length above his head. A mighty roar came up out of the black man's deep chest as he threw Anello.

Hurtling through the air, Anello hit the ground at speed, his body rolling in several revolutions before coming to rest, the breath knocked out of it.

Seeing the negro running toward him, Anello came up onto his knees, reaching for a shovel left lying around by one of the nuns. Scooping dust, dirt and gravel onto the blade, Anello tossed it into the face of the black man with a flick of the handle of the shovel. Still winded, Anello got shakily to his feet as the negro used both hands to desperately try to rub the grit from sore eyes.

Taking advantage of his formidable opponent being temporarily out of action, Anello swung the shovel, the blade side-on in a slicing movement, at the black man's right knee. The negro screamed shrilly as the kneecap was shattered. Doing the same to the left knee, possibly harder and with even more agonizing effect, Anello laid down the shovel in the belief that with the handicap of two smashed patellas, the superhumanly strong negro and himself were now evenly matched.

Wading into the black man, who was standing awkwardly in the way of a child that has wet itself, Anello drove in four hard punches to the belly, left and right, left and right. In return he took a clubbing, stunning right, but when he attacked once more with body punches, and the black man tried to grab and hold him, Anello drove an uppercut that connected to knock the black man's head back violently. Eyes rolling whitely, the negro collapsed to the ground on his face.

The black man started to get up, having problems because of his broken knees. Fists clenched, Anello stood ready for him. The negro looked slyly at him while still in a crouch, then reached out quickly to seize the length of timber with which he had first felled Anello.

With the black man ready to spring at him swinging the lethal, improvised club, Anello decided that enough was enough. Picking up the shovel he held it at arm's length while bringing it and his body round in one power-packed movement. The flat of the metal blade struck the back of the negro's head with a bone-crushing, dull clunk. The huge man dropped to the ground, the back of his skull completely smashed in.

Slumping onto the stump of a tree, Anello sat for a while with his head bowed, allowing his strength to return. Then he stood. There was not a nun in sight. They had run into the dormitory at the start of the fight, closing and securing the door. One at a time, he draped the bodies of the three men over the backs of their horses, securing them by tying wrists to ankles under the bellies of the animals. He would take them with him, bury them along the way, and turn the horses loose.

Checking the ground, he used the shovel to cover

some blood with dust – blood that had leaked from the two men he had shot, the scar-faced man in particular. In a final clearing up to save the nuns from distress, he scooped up some grey brain matter that had spilled out of the negro's split-open skull. Carrying it some way on the shovel, he tossed it into a concealing crevice. Then he led the three horses, made skittish by the smell of blood and the corpses on their backs, to hitch them in a cluster of trees, out of sight of those in the Mission.

Walking back, Anello saw the door of the dormitory open as he approached. Sister Joseph, neat and tidy once more, but ashen-faced, came out and closed the door behind her. She came to stand in front of Anello, so close that she had to tilt her head back to look up at him.

Face serious, she spoke very quietly. 'I am grateful to you for saving us, Mr Anello.'

'Would you believe me, Sister Joseph, if I say that I regret the measures I had to take to do so?' he asked, finding himself anxiously awaiting her answer.

'I know what is in your heart, that which makes the real you,' she said. 'What is in your head is what others have put there. You are a soldier, Mr Anello, am I right?'

Taken aback, he gasped, 'How could you know that?'

'I'm not able to work miracles,' she assured him, permitting a smile to fleetingly brighten her face. 'It can be seen in your manner, the proud way in which you hold yourself.'

'I am not a deserter,' he told her, anxious to separate himself from the countless scum who were on the run from the armies of both sides.

'That is the last thing I would think of you,' she smiled again. 'I take it that you must now be on your way?'

Anello nodded, doing a quarter turn, asking before he walked away from her, 'Can I maybe come back one day, Sister Joseph?'

Putting a small, slim-fingered hand on his arm, taking a pinch of the material of his shirt between thumb and forefinger, she looked deeply into his eyes.

'If you cannot free yourself from the hate that you carry with you, Mr Anello,' she said, 'then do come back one day and, with God's help, I will help you release it.'

Nodding assent, Anello closed a hand over the cool one she still had on his arm. Ashamed at the liberty he had taken, he took his hand away. His voice had a tremor to it as he said, 'Goodbye, Sister Joseph.'

'Goodbye,' she said softly.

Their eyes stayed together up to the last moment when he forced himself to turn his back on her and walk away.

'Mr Anello!'

Anello stopped, waiting for her to go on, still facing away from her.

'Please don't ever come back for any other reason,' she said pleadingly.

'Are you sure?' he asked, turning to face her.

Taking a long time to reply, she then answered, 'I have to be.'

Having said that, she turned quickly and hurried back to the dormitory. Not moving, Anello watched her go. Not until she went inside the wooden building, without once looking back, and had closed the door behind her, did he walk away toward his horse.

Two

'Rider coming up on us, Pa!'

Lonnie Morrow had been standing in the stirrups, taking a look behind him. A lone horseman was approaching at a steady lope across the rugged, barren terrain. Now, after calling to his father, the rancher's son dropped back down into the saddle, wheeling his horse around to spur it through the chaparral to assist one of the hands edge a young steer that was about to bolt, back into the herd.

'Let him come,' Matthew Morrow yelled to his son, turning a weathered, worried face to the swollen river ahead of his herd. 'If'n he wants to sign on, we could use another hand crossing the Red.'

'Best see what sort he is first. He may not be no use to us, Pa.'

The old man liked this streak of caution in his son. Most of the young men around had that kind of wildness that invited danger. Lonnie, built like a bull and with the strength to tackle anything that might come his way, was a level-headed young man who could handle any kind of crisis.

Epitaph of Vengeance 37

'He must have something going for him,' Matthew Morrow commented as he rode to the side of his son, the two of them watching the stranger come ahead, 'or he sure wouldn't have gotten through Indian Territory all on his lonesome.'

The rider came on. The hard look of him went with the territory and didn't surprise the two waiting men. In their minds, both dismissed the idea that he might be a gunslinger. With a holstered Colt riding low on his thigh, the newcomer might well have been except for the fact he lacked the latent viciousness that experience had taught the Morrows to look for. Neither was he a saddle-tramp down on his luck. His clothing was worn but cared for, and he sat in the saddle with the pride of a Comanche chief.

'I sure can't figure this one out,' Lonnie Morrow puzzled in a low tone as the newcomer reined up in front of his father and himself. Lonnie raised his voice. 'You looking for work, stranger?'

Not replying, the alert-eyed stranger took in everything around him, the herd being held in tight check by too few cowboys, and the flooded river the cattle were being pushed toward. Then he brought his gaze back to the father and son as he finally answered, 'That depends.'

'On what?' Matthew Morrow asked gruffly, unaccustomed to range riders being so independently choosy.

'On where you're driving that beef, mister.'

'That herd is going to feed the Southern army,' Lonnie answered.

Nodding acceptance of this, the stranger gave it some careful thought, then enquired, 'Are you hiring?'

'That depends,' the father said flatly.

'On what?' the newcomer asked, having the tables turned on him bringing a twinkle of amusement to his eyes.

'On whether you're a Yankee,' Matthew Morrow said pointedly enough to warn the stranger off.

'Right now I'm not anything,' the newcomer said, leaning forward to soothingly pat the neck of his suddenly restless chestnut horse.

'That's only half an answer, *hombre*,' Lonnie Morrow complained.

'Maybe so,' the stranger shrugged wide shoulders, 'but it's all you're going to get.'

The father and son exchanged questioning looks. Each wanted the other to make the decision. They could well use an extra hand. They were close to desperate enough to take on some Cherokee, but they'd learned before that while some of the Cherokee were working for you, unfriendly Indians hovered menacingly in the vicinity.

It was the older man who took on the hiring responsibility. 'You any good at riding herd?'

'I'm pretty good at most things, mister.'

'Except giving direct answers to questions,' Lonnie Morrow remarked.

Lifting his reins, the newcomer told him, 'If you don't like what I say, fella, then I guess I'll be on my way.'

'Hold on there, don't be so hasty!' the older man said. 'There's a whole heap of difference to trailing a herd and crossing a river like this here when short handed. We used to keep a couple of swimming steers to lead the others. Used to bring them back and forth, regular like. Lost the pair of them in the Mississippi shortly after those bad rains in '60. Sure was a blow, that.'

'There's one way to find out if I can do it, mister, and that's try me,' the newcomer suggested.

Turning this over in his mind, the rancher said, 'I'm prepared to take you on trial. You help us making the crossing, and if you know your stuff, you're hired for the rest of the drive. If'n you don't come up to scratch, then I'll pay you for your time and we'll say *adios*.'

'That's a fair enough offer,' the rider agreed to the terms.

'Right,' the rancher said. 'Let's get moving. I'm Matthew Morrow, and this here's my son, Lonnie.'

Moving his horse forward, the rider shook the hands of both of them, saying, 'I'm August Anello.'

'You're heartily welcome,' Matthew Morrow said. 'I'll take the point. With the water high it ain't going to be easy starting the beef across. Lonnie, take Anello on the right flank with you and Garcia. Let's get started.'

The cattle protested noisily as they pushed them toward the water. There had been a lot of rain and the river was swollen. It was not the raging torrent it occasionally was, but all crossings held problems, most of them unexpected. Not willing to follow Matthew Morrow, who was swimming his horse across ahead of them, the cows had to be driven. Consequently, they tried to break away at the flanks, which meant that Lonnie, Anello, and Garcia, a young *vaquero*, were hard pressed to contain the herd as they entered the water. The three hands on the opposite flank were experiencing the same trouble.

It got easier when the lead cows had made a start and Anello and the others were swimming their horses beside the cattle. But there was a strong current a third of the way across that had the water break in hissing little white waves around the riders and cows, increasing the nervousness of the latter.

With the swirling of the water and the bellowing of the cattle, the noise reached a crescendo that would frighten and confuse anyone other than experienced cowhands. But it was going well. Riding behind Lonnie, Anello was kept busy as cows that had been pushed back into line by the rancher's son had another try at breaking away.

It was Garcia, the Mexican, who first saw the danger and cried out a warning. Anello spotted what had alarmed the *vaquero*. Floating downstream on a course that would take it across in front of the herd, twisting and twirling as it came, was a huge log.

As it came near the lead cattle they began to turn back and circle upon themselves. Matthew Morrow was shouting at them, cursing, cajoling, trying to have them start forwards again, but it was wasted effort. With no choice but to put themselves in peril, the cowboys, yelling and yipping, swam their horses among clashing, piercing horns. The cattle had to be brought under control, for already three of them were being washed downriver to certain deaths by drowning. Anello fought the cows beside Lonnie and the Mexican. It was tough going, but, very gradually, they were gaining the upper hand.

Then disaster struck. A terrified cow with a spread of at least six feet between the two points of its horns, tried to scramble over the backs of other cows. In its lunging it gored Lonnie Morrow's right thigh, thrusting the horn in deep to the bone, knocking the man out of the saddle into the river.

Forcing his horse through the muddy water that was already reddened by blood from Lonnie's deep injury, Anello made slow progress toward him through the milling cattle. Aware of what had happened, the father was trying to get back to where his son was in trouble, but it was impossible for him to make it. Anello watched Lonnie weakly reach for the tail of his horse. Grabbing the tail of his horse or a cow was the only hope for an unsaddled rider in the river. It was even more vital for a man who was injured. Fingers missing the tail by inches, the rancher's son sank beneath the water. Lonnie didn't resurface.

Sliding from his saddle, Anello kept hold of the reins of his horse with one hand as he went under the water. Buffeted by the panicking cattle, only luck had him avoid flailing hoofs. Peering through the brownish semi-darkness of the water, eyes stinging, he spotted Lonnie Morrow through the wildly threshing legs of the cattle.

Just a few feet from him, the rancher's son was floating just above the bed of the river, arms and legs outstretched. Holding his breath, lungs straining, Anello was almost forced to exhale when the knee of a cow slammed hard into his ribs. Grasping the right wrist of Lonnie Morrow, pulling him close through the water, Anello got an arm round the man and struggled toward the surface. It was then he realized he'd lost his grip on the reins and his horse had swum off, deserting him.

His chest giving him intense pain now, feeling as if it was about to explode, Anello could see daylight far above him, the pattern of ripples telling him that it was the surface. His one-armed upward swimming, made even more difficult by the heavy body of Lonnie, told him that he would not make it. Releasing the unconscious man would enable Anello to save himself, but not for one moment did he consider this.

It was the end! Feeling consciousness slipping away, Anello knew that he was about to lose power over his breathing. Within seconds he would be filling his lungs with foul river water. Would he be meeting Silver Moon? This possibility sustained him, and then he saw an image of the lovely Sister Joseph and he raked through his boyhood memories, trying to dig a remembered prayer from under the debris of passing years.

Surrendering to his fate, Anello was about to bring

Epitaph of Vengeance 43

welcome relief to his lungs, fully aware of the dire consequences, when his shoulder bumped against something and he felt hands reaching for Lonnie and himself. Muffled voices came to him. Realizing that the current had miraculously taken him to the riverbank, Anello felt hands reaching under the water for Lonnie and himself. Then they were pulled out and he lay on the bank drawing deep breaths as Lonnie Morrow was pulled from him.

Getting up onto his feet, sliding on the mud, Anello saw Garcia and Matthew Morrow turn the half-drowned Lonnie on his side. Muddy water gushed out of his mouth, and Anello stopped worrying when he heard Lonnie cough and splutter. Turning his attention to the river, he took in a scene of total chaos. The Morrows' remaining four cowboys had distanced themselves from the cows they had lost control of.

'The herd!' Anello shouted as the cattle threshed about in the water, the four remaining cowboys staying back for safety, having no control over the cows.

'We'll have to lose them,' an anxious Morrow called to him. 'My son's life is more important.'

Agreeing with this, Anello pulled off his neckerchief as he knelt beside Lonnie, and tied it around the thigh above the gaping wound inflicted by the horn. Reaching to take a narrow-bladed knife from Garcia, Anello thrust it under the *bandana* and twisted the knife to make a tourniquet. He was watching the bleeding slow when the drumming of unshod hoofs caught his attention. Turning quickly, Anello stood up as a band of ten Cherokee rode up to sit on their ponies looking down at them.

Putting Matthew Morrow's hand on the tourniquet, Anello instructed, 'Ease that off every few minutes, then tighten it again.'

Standing, he looked to where his bedraggled horse stood shivering, yards away. His gunbelt and gun were wrapped round the saddle horn where he had put them before entering the water. His rifle was there, too. Resigned to being unarmed, Anello looked up at a Cherokee, who was dark-visaged but had a look of intelligence about him. The Indian seemed willing either to fight if Anello and the others wanted it that way, or be friendly if that suited the white men.

Anello gestured to where the cattle fought and floundered in the water, several of them floating downriver after having drowned. Looking at the herd, the Cherokee gave a curt nod, then made a sign that asked what reward was on offer.

'Ten!' Anello mimed, holding up both hands with all fingers and thumbs extended.

Giving him a disdainful look, the Indian raised both of his hands twice in rapid succession. His payment for helping get the now totally disorganized herd across the river would be twenty of the cows. It was a simple matter of losing the whole herd or giving away twenty longhorns. Matthew Morrow was still tending to his injured son, so Anello made the decision for him by signing to the Cherokee that they had a deal.

Fetching his horse, Anello mounted up and coaxed the animal back into life. Riding into the river amid the struggling cattle, he took charge. Anello directed the Cherokee who, as expert horsemen, turned the cattle and shaped them back into raggedy columns heading toward the northern bank of the river.

When the herd was once again on dry land and the Morrows' cowhands were able to keep them together, the Cherokee leader instructed his braves which twenty cows he wanted. When the Indians had rounded them up, their leader made a sign of friendship to Anello, who gave a like reply. Then the Cherokee rode off without a word having been exchanged.

Lonnie Morrow, as strong as a horse, his leg bandaged, was standing unaided when Anello rode back and dismounted. A grateful Matthew Morrow told Anello, 'We owe you just about everything, son. Rest assured, we'll see to it that you get your dues for what you've done.'

'Just the same wages as the other hands are getting will suit me fine, Morrow,' Anello said as Lonnie, limping a little, came over to silently shake him by the hand.

'We'll see about that,' the rancher replied, squinting at heavy clouds up ahead, so dark that they blurred the horizon. 'My boy says that he's fit to ride, so I guess we'd better keep going. We've got three days' hard drive ahead of us afore we reach where them soldiers are camped.'

They made it quicker than that. Pushing on through two and a half days of torrential rain, made anonymous by the yellow oilskin slickers they wore, eating little, sleeping less, they arrived at the tented camp of the Confederate army.

It staggered Anello to view the sea of tents that covered a vast area of land. Estimating that there had to be some forty thousand men in the camp, he knew that this gathering of troops had to be a part of a massive campaign. What he saw didn't unnerve him, but it was a strange feeling to be riding toward an enemy camp. Sounds that he recognized were reaching him. There were shouted orders, the palm of the hand against a wooden stock smacking sounds of musketry drill, and the lesser noises, the clinking of mess tins, a yelled curse, and a snatch or two of song. None of these things was the prerogative of any one army, and for the first time Anello fully realized that the soldier on one side in a war was the same as the soldier on the other side. Only the uniforms differed.

With the rain still teeming down, and with thunder and lightning a possibility, the highly strung herd could stampede at any time. So they halted the cattle half a mile outside of the camp. Matthew Morrow rode out of the grey mist of falling rain to Anello's side.

'The ride's been tough on Lonnie,' the rancher shouted at Anello above the drumming, hissing rain. 'I'd be mighty grateful if you would ride on ahead and let them know we're here.'

Waving a hand to indicate that he would do as

Epitaph of Vengeance

he'd been asked, Anello headed for the camp at a steady pace, his horse splashing through the mud, keeping its head down as a protection against the rain. He passed through a perimeter of tents without challenge, but was then stopped by a sentry who held a Springfield rifle on him. There was no real threat to Anello in the situation. His own army had Springfields and he knew they were accurate at long distances. But this close, in the atrocious conditions, the sentinel was likely to miss with his first shot, and the complex loading procedure limited the most skilled rifleman to two shots per minute.

'State your business here, sir!' the Confederate soldier challenged, rain streaming down his face, and his edginess evident in his stance.

'We're bringing in a herd of beef,' Anello replied. 'My business is with your supply officer.'

'I don't know who the supply officer is. . . .' the sentry began uncertainly, but a figure wearing a rain-sodden uniform marked with the insignia of a lieutenant loomed like a phantom out of the rain to take over from him.

'I'll take care of this, soldier,' the officer said, looking up at Anello, a friendly smile on his young, pleasant face. 'Welcome, friend. It's been tough here in this weather, but I guess you sure had it a lot worse out on the trail. You fellows can't give up, but we've got more men in company Q than we have serving here.'

Aware that 'company Q' was what the Confederate army called its sick list, Anello didn't let on that he knew. A trail-driver as he was supposed to be wouldn't have the slightest idea. He said, 'Once I find your supply officer I'll be able to dry myself out a bit.'

'I'll take you to him,' the Confederate officer said, 'but I'd sure take it kindly if you'd join me in a couple of glasses of tanglefoot first. I sure could use a talk with somebody who's not spouting military facts and figures. I'm Lieutenant Jonathan Forrest. Follow me, friend, we've got a mess, of sorts.'

Leaning down from the saddle, Anello took the hand proffered by the friendly lieutenant and shook it, giving his name, 'August Anello.' Then he rode slowly in the wake of Forrest, hunch-shouldered as he plodded through the rain, who led him to a large tent so water-logged that it was sagging out of shape.

Dismounting, Anello went cautiously into the tent with the Confederate lieutenant. The presence of a civilian was bound to cause a stir, and he didn't want questions asked about him. So far he had no plan. He had covered the early ground in his mission by getting himself into a Confederate camp. From now on he had to play his tune of vengeance by ear.

The interior of the big tent, with a bar at one end and a collection of occupied tables and chairs, bore a resemblance to officers' messes everywhere, but this one was makeshift to the point of being unstable as the rain drummed against the canvas.

At the bar, Forrest ordered whiskey for Anello and himself. Although his entrance had caused no more than a mild stir of interest among the officers who were sitting around drinking, Anello felt threatened,

Epitaph of Vengeance 49

without being able to discover why this should be.

'Here's to whatever General E. Lee's got planned for us,' Lieutenant Forrest said with a grin, raising his glass. 'Whatever it is, it's something pretty big, August, and I'm sure pleased we'll be marching on full bellies now that you've brought them beeves here.'

Anello raised his glass. 'Here's to you, Lieutenant Forrest, for showing a poor pilgrim such hospitality on a bad night.'

'Call me Jonathan,' Forrest protested. 'It's my pleasure. Strangers are scarcer than hens' teeth around here. Now, tell me what's going on in the world outside of parading, cleaning weapons and polishing boots.'

'Life's just going on like it always has,' Anello replied, amused because he hadn't long been out of the kind of environment the lieutenant was complaining about. Draining his glass, he invited his companion, 'Drink up, Jonathan. It's my turn to pay.'

'No, put your cash away, August,' Forrest objected, looking carefully around him and lowering his voice. 'Confederate money is worthless, friend, so why should you waste the real stuff? Are you the owner of the herd you brought all this long way, August?'

'Just a hired hand,' Anello shook his head.

'I'm glad to hear that, because your boss is going to be paid with money that wouldn't buy five minutes with a diseased gal in a bawdy house,' Forrest warned Anello before calling to a barman, 'More drinks here, boy, quick as you like.'

Idly glancing at the large, cropped head of the barman, Anello felt a jolt of half recognition. Now he began to understand where his feeling of dread had come from. There was something familiar about the face with its beaked nose, and the two widely spaced, protruding teeth. At first he couldn't put a name to it: then he had it, Hemsford. Until some nine months ago this man had served in Anello's outfit. He had been known as a copperhead then – a Northerner who sympathized with the Southern cause. When Hemsford, a useless soldier, had deserted Anello had been relieved.

Now, as he poured drinks, Hemsford was eyeing Anello in his sly manner. Aware that he was on dangerous ground, for he didn't doubt that Hemsford had recognized him, Anello downed his latest drink and told Forrest, 'I'd better see that supply officer, or my boss'll be after my guts.'

'Just one more drink,' Forrest begged. 'We haven't really talked yet, August. You wouldn't spoil a lonely, bored Southern soldier's pleasure, would you?'

'Just one more,' Anello relented while suspecting that he might well regret delaying here.

'I promise,' Forrest put his hand on his heart before signalling to Hemsford for more drinks, 'your man will still be in his tent, working away. He's one of those career officers who's as dead as a can of corned beef. I often tell him that he'll stop being ambitious when eighteen inches of Yankee bayonet are rammed into his guts. But John Peck never listens to sense.'

Epitaph of Vengeance 51

As Forrest spoke the name, it was highlighted on the list that Anello carried in his mind. He couldn't believe the luck that had him find the Morrows so that he would come here and find one of the Confederate officers who had killed Silver Moon.

Covering his impatience, Anello drank the last drink with Forrest. He somehow managed to carry on a conversation that interested his companion, even though Anello didn't really know what he was saying. Then at last they were out in the rain again, splashing along until they reached a bell tent. Stopping, Forrest leaned close to Anello to say, 'I'll just put my head in and announce who you are. Peck is the kind of fellow I do my best to avoid.'

Putting his head in the flap of the tent, Forrest brought it out quickly and held the flap for Anello to enter, saying, 'If you've time when you've done your business, you'll find me in the mess, August.'

'I'll do my best,' Anello replied, although he knew that he wouldn't. 'Thanks for your help, and the drinks, Jonathan.'

Stepping inside the tent he saw a Confederate officer sitting behind two ammunition boxes that had been stacked on top of each other. Spread out on them were papers that Anello could see were invoices and bills of sale. When the officer stood to greet him, Anello noticed that his seat had been another ammunition box.

Lieutenant John Peck was in his mid-thirties. Of less than average height and as lean as a starving man, he extended a bony hand to Anello. When

Peck gave what he probably regarded as a smile, he showed yellow top teeth that sloped drastically inwards. Having to push himself into taking the hand that had played a part in murdering his beloved Osage girl, Anello knew what he must do. His left hand moved surreptitiously to the handle of the knife pushed into his belt. Before breaking the handshake he would produce the knife and drive it into Peck. He would be on his horse and out of the camp before anyone was the wiser. It was rough on the two Morrows, who he had come to like, but they would have to make their own arrangements to pass over the herd.

Peck sensed something. Seeing the Confederate's eyes change, Anello was tightening his grip on the officer's hand when the tent flap was pulled open and a voice commanded, 'Hold it right there!'

Turning, Anello found himself facing a moustachioed captain holding a pistol. Beside the captain stood a sergeant and a private soldier, both holding rifles trained on Anello. Behind the Confederates, lurking in the shadows at the edge of the light thrown by the oil lamp standing on Peck's ammunition boxes, was Hemsford. Seeing the former Union soldier, Anello knew the worst before the captain spoke.

'This man is an officer in the Union army, Lieutenant Peck,' the captain told a startled supply officer. Then he stepped forward, staying out of line of the two rifles, to press the muzzle of his revolver hard into Anello's back, confirming that Hemsford had a good memory by using Anello's name as he announced, 'You are under arrest, Lieutenant Anello. Not as a prisoner-of-war, no, sir, but as a Union spy.'

Three

With no way of measuring passing time in the darkness, Anello knew only that it had been a very long night. He estimated that at least four hours had gone by since he had seen anyone. Captain Haining, the officer who had arrested him in Peck's tent, had said it was midnight when he had arrived to tell Anello that General Lee had approved and signed the order that he be put to death by musketry at dawn. Haining had made a great play on a death of infamy before a firing squad for a Union officer. Expecting some response from Anello, and not getting one because death was final, and it mattered little how a man met it, the captain had left. Since then Anello had only the rain drumming on the canvas, and the pacing of the sentry outside for company. Tied to the centre pole of the tent, he had slid down to half squat, half sit on the floor. It was far from comfortable but not so much of a strain on his whole body as standing up had been.

He had constantly berated himself for making a direct approach to Lieutenant Peck. Once he had discovered the supply officer's identity from Jonathan Forrest, he should have sneaked to the tent, done the job and left. He had failed and in doing so had denied Silver Moon her right to revenge. Now John Peck would never suffer from knowing how close he had come to death. The supply officer hadn't even learned why Anello was there. It would be easier for Anello to face the firing squad at dawn if he had at least put some fear into Peck.

From outside the tent came the sound of muffled voices. Anello assumed that the guard was being changed. Since being tied up in here he had added Hemsford's name to the death list in his head. That had been a satisfying but pointless exercise. When he died in the morning that personal list would fade away forever.

Unable to see because it was so dark, he felt a cold, moist draught that told him the flap had been lifted. Then it returned to being humid inside the tent. The flap had closed again, but Anello felt sure that there was someone inside the tent with him.

'Who's that?' Anello questioned in a sibilant whisper.

'Keep your voice down, it's Lonnie Morrow,' Morrow spoke from close by as his hand made a fumbling exploration of the ropes that bound Anello to the pole.

A surge of relief went through Anello until he realized the chance the rancher's son was taking. He whispered some urgent advice. 'Get out of here,

Lonnie. If they find you they'll shoot you as a spy the same as they're going to do to me. Get away while you can. Leave me!'

'Like you left me at the bottom of the river,' Lonnie said tellingly as he sawed through Anello's bonds with a knife.

'How did you know I was here?'

Welcoming the move to free him, although both Lonnie and himself had yet to get out of the camp, Anello was puzzled by what was happening. The Morrows were waiting some way from the camp expecting his return. So how did Lonnie know what had happened to him?

'A Confederate officer rode out and told us,' Lonnie Morrow replied. Having cut Anello's hands free he was now kneeling at his feet, cursing the pain in his injured leg as he cut the ropes round Anello's ankles. 'He said you are a drinking companion of his and that you were in big trouble. Said it was more than his life was worth to help you directly, so he explained to me where you were. He wouldn't even give us his name.'

The name was Jonathan Forrest, Anello knew. The young officer was a real decent kind. The two of them had been made enemies by politics but had become friends by choice. It made a nonsense of everything.

'What did you do with the guard outside?' a mystified Anello asked. He had heard only a short conversation, no sounds of a scuffle.

Lonnie gave a little chuckle as he cut the final

strand of ropes to free Anello's ankles. 'On a night like this it didn't take much to persuade him to desert. I gave him a fistful of money and a promise that he could ride back to Texas with us and have a job on our ranch. Last I saw of him he was mounted up and heading out to where we've bedded down the herd.'

Rubbing his wrists and twisting his ankles round to get his circulation back into proper operation, Anello was ready to leave. They had to get away before a sentry came to relieve the one that Lonnie had bribed.

'I brought you a horse,' Lonnie said when they were outside the tent in the slashing rain. 'That officer said how they'd taken yours. We better ride out of here real slow and quiet like.'

Standing at Lonnie's side by the two horses, Anello put a hand on the shoulder of the man who had rescued him, saying, 'You ride out ahead, Lonnie. I've got a couple of things to do, then I'll follow you.'

Nodding, sending rainwater cascading from the wide brim of his stetson, Lonnie Morrow reached for the reins of his horse. Peering through the gloom, an unhappy expression on his face, he said, 'Seems to me, Anello, that you ain't likely to be riding out to join us. I allow that we won't never see each other again.'

'Never's a real long time, Lonnie,' Anello said.

The two of them shook hands as a lone streak of lightning split the sky brightly well to the north. Mounting up, Lonnie Morrow moved slowly off, heading out of the camp. Spending a minute or two watching him go, Anello then turned and crept a zigzag course through the tents on foot. He remembered seeing a bedroll in the corner of Peck's tent. That suggested that the supply officer slept at his place of work. The lieutenant was about to get a visit that he wouldn't like.

To get himself orientated, Anello went back to the hulking black silhouette of the now closed officers' mess. From there memory helped him find his way to Lieutenant Peck's tent. There were no sentries in this area. Anello guessed that the Confederates' military commanders were sure they had nothing to fear this far from any Union forces, and were resting their troops in preparation for some large-scale campaign.

Reaching the tent he found the flap secured from inside. Taking his razor-sharp knife from his belt, Anello slid it in through the slit and noiselessly cut the cords holding the flap shut. Crouching, he moved inside, stopping cautiously, hunkering on his heels as he listened to hear if he had disturbed Peck. A steady, heavy breathing that was close to snoring came from where he had earlier seen the bedroll. Moving across to it, eyes adjusting to the poor light inside the tent, Anello made out the prone figure of a sleeping man.

Knife held in his right hand, he pounced, clapping his left hand over Peck's mouth, holding him down, keeping him mute as he let the point of his knife prick through the skin of the Confederate officer's neck, close to the main artery. Then he took his hand away from the mouth, keeping the knife in place.

'Who are you?' an indignant Peck asked. 'What is going on. I shall call for the guard!'

Moving the knife just a little, aware that he was drawing blood while causing pain, Anello said, 'Raise your voice above a whisper, Peck, and I'll slit your throat from ear to ear.'

'You're that damned Union officer from yesterday evening!' Peck exclaimed. 'What do you want from me?'

'Me? I don't want anything, Peck. A young Indian girl asked me to call on you.'

'What are you talking about?' a puzzled Peck asked angrily. 'I'm going to get up!'

Not answering verbally, Anello dug his knife in a little deeper to convince the Confederate officer that he should lie still. He was pleased to detect a tremor in Peck's voice as the Confederate complained, 'What's all this horseshit about an Indian girl having sent you.'

'Well. . . .' Anello began with mock humility, 'I wasn't exactly telling the truth there, Lieutenant. It was this Osage girl's ghost that told me you, Captain Witsell and lieutenants Woodward, Mallory, Siegle and Mack killed her.'

'I had no part in that,' Peck protested. 'Me and Captain Witsell tried to stop the others. The Indians killed the captain, and I managed to escape. I had nothing to do with what happened to the girl, I swear it!'

Anello, able to smell both Peck's sweat and his fear, each every bit as distinct as the other, was enjoying himself. Inside his head he could see Silver Moon, sweet and innocent, smiling the welcoming smile she once saved especially for him. Peck increased Anello's keen anticipation of revenge by starting to beg for his life.

'I can tell you where the others are! The guilty ones! The men you really want,' the Confederate was blabbering. 'Antony Siegle has left the army. He took a bullet in the leg at Chancellorsville. He's gone back to farming with his wife, a Mexican. The rest of them are all with General Lee's headquarters, getting ready for the big push north.'

An easing of the blackness of night warned Anello that he had little time left. Sensing the urgency in the man holding a knife to his throat, Lieutenant Peck sobbed as he pleaded, 'I don't want to die!'

'Neither did that Osage girl,' Anello countered bitterly, suddenly overcome by hatred.

Silver Moon would not want this man to die quickly and relatively painlessly. Clamping a hand tightly over Peck's mouth to prevent him from screaming or groaning, Anello took the knife from his throat and drove it deep into the Confederate's belly, dragging it up through until the blade struck hard against the breastbone, feeling the convulsions of agony jerking at the dying man's body.

Removing the knife and wiping it clean on Peck's bedroll, Anello felt a revulsion at his own act. It was a nauseating sensation that stubbornly refused to

Epitaph of Vengeance

leave him. Lacking the ability to move, Anello could only stand still inside the tent, risking recapture, until Silver Moon came into his mind and pushed the bad feeling away. Remembering her, Anello accepted that Peck deserved to die. The Confederate officer merited a worse death than the one he had suffered.

Going out of the tent into the first greyness of a new day, Anello paused for a moment, looking around him to identify the tent to which he had been taken on being arrested the previous night. It looked to be used as an office and store, so he was fairly confident that no soldiers slept there. Keeping close to the other tents so as not to stand out should a sentry suddenly appear, he found the flap open and went in. There was enough light for him to see his gunbelt and holstered gun lying on top of a crate. Slinging the belt around his waist, Anello buckled it on, then drew his gun and checked the chambers. It had been emptied. His expensive saddle and rifle were not to be seen. He assumed that both had been stolen by a Confederate soldier or soldiers. Going to the tent opening, keeping a wary eye outside, he loaded the Colt. Sliding the six-shooter back into its holster, he went out to make his way to where Lonnie Morrow had left the horse for him.

There was no one about as he made his stealthy way through the camp. Anello was surprised by the air of laxity around him. Things were very different in the Union army. Reveille would have sounded by now and the routine of the day started in earnest.

Epitaph of Vengeance

With only a short distance to go to the horse, Anello was rounding the back of the officers' mess when a trooper stepped out in front of him. Both were equally startled, but Anello was the first to recover. Grabbing what he discovered was a private soldier, he threw him to the ground onto his back, and dropped to pin him down with a knee on his chest. Drawing his knife with the intention of finishing off the Confederate, Anello stayed his hand as he found himself looking down into the terrified face of Hemsford.

'Please, Captain Anello!' Hemsford pleaded.

Always immature, the former Union soldier had now reverted to a snivelling child. With every reason to kill Hemsford, who was a deserter from the Union army as well as the Judas who had betrayed him to the Confederates last evening, Anello found himself unable to drive his knife home. Yet there was really no alternative. To let Hemsford live would mean the boy raising the alarm. If that happened, then Anello would be shot down before he could get out of the camp. It was a case of either Hemsford's life or his own. Although starkly aware of that fact, Anello still couldn't kill the boy.

It was Hemsford who offered a solution of sorts. Terror-stricken eyes going from the knife to Anello, his thick bottom lip quivering, he said squeakily, 'Get away, Captain Anello, sir. Get away from here while you can. I won't say nothing, I promise, sir, I promise!'

Hemsford's word wasn't to be relied upon, but the

situation didn't leave Anello with any choice. Replacing his knife in his belt, he got up off Hemsford with a threatening, 'Open your mouth, boy, and I'll be back to slit your throat before they get me.'

'I won't say nothing, Captain Anello, sir,' the boy gulped.

There were sounds of activity somewhere distant in the camp now. This urged Anello on as he ran to where the saddled horse waited. Swinging up onto its back, he sent the horse off at a gallop, telling himself that either he had misjudged Hemsford, or the boy had been too frightened of him to raise the alarm.

About fifty yards from the edge of the camp he discovered he'd been wrong on both counts. Behind him there was much shouting and the blowing of whistles. Hemsford had betrayed him yet again. Spurring the horse hard, he knew that he wouldn't live long if captured. Already sentenced to death as a spy, he would receive no mercy when Lieutenant John Peck's sliced-open body was found in his tent.

Out of the camp now, galloping across terrain that was still muddy despite the heavy rain having stopped sometime during the night, Anello glanced over his shoulder and his heart sank. A line of Confederate riflemen were on one knee, Springfields raised to their shoulders. At this distance, some three hundred yards, those weapons, their slugs imparted with a spin as they left the barrel, were deadly accurate.

He heard the crackling of the rifles echoing on

the early-morning air. Unable to believe his luck, Anello rode on unhurt, completely untouched. Just fifty yards ahead was a rocky area where he could easily lose any mounted Confederates who might come after him. Heading for those rocks, he feared the worst when his horse faltered, just once, before carrying on as strongly as ever. With only a few yards to go, he patted the neck of the animal encouragingly, just as the horse collapsed completely under him and he went over its head to hit the ground, rolling with the fall.

Splattered with mud, he knelt up to look back at the horse. It was a miracle that it had got him this far. Instinct alone, perhaps together with some kind of reflex action, had kept the horse going. The soft lead minie ball from a Springfield rifle, though only half an inch in diameter and one inch long, had a hollow base that had expanded on impact to bloodily tear away much of the horse's left flank.

A glance back at the Confederate camp told Anello that, as yet, no detail had been ordered to ride out after him. Pleased that this afforded him the opportunity to make it to the rocks, where he could conceal himself, he got to his feet.

Shaking the wet mud from his clothing to free himself of the hindering weight of it, Anello raised his head to see two Indians on horseback looking down at him, their lances raised. They were Choctaw, and they looked mean as they moved their ponies each side of Anello, hemming him in.

On foot and vulnerable, with the Indians sitting

Epitaph of Vengeance 65

their ponies side-on to him, Anello backed away from the threat of one Choctaw, only to come up against the pony of the other. He let his right hand stray slowly towards his holstered Colt, but the Indian in front of him noticed and raised his lance a little. Not making another move, Anello realized that the only reason he was still alive was because the Choctaw intended to have some fun before killing him.

Aware that he had to do something, and do it fast, Anello took a step toward the Indian in front of him. Expecting some attempt at an attack, the Choctaw raise his lance, ready to spear Anello. But Anello dropped swiftly onto his backside on the ground, lifting his feet and legs high to roll backwards between the front and back legs of the Indian pony behind him. Quick though Anello was, the Choctaw showed superior reflexes. As Anello, knife in hand, came up off the ground, so did the Choctaw come down off his pony, his lance held firmly, aimed at Anello.

Changing direction as he came up onto his feet, Anello felt the tip of the Choctaw lance slice through the shoulder of his coat. Swinging his knife arm in at the Indian's chest, Anello learned just how fast the Choctaw was when he was made to miss, his blade bringing a gush of blood from his opponent's left arm as it slashed across it.

Dropping the lance, the Choctaw drew a knife and sprang at Anello. Each holding the wrist of the other's knife hand, they rolled over and over in the mud, with the other Choctaw, still mounted, moving his pony this way and that in the hope of getting a clear thrust at Anello with his lance.

Kneed in the groin by the Indian he was grappling with, Anello was in so much pain that he came close to losing his grip on the wrist. Knowing well that he was facing an accomplished fighter, Anello had no compunction in scooping up a handful of wet mud in his free hand and smearing it across and into the Choctaw's eyes. Releasing the Indian, Anello sprang to his feet. The Choctaw came up in a crouching position, still holding the knife, blinded by the mud that he was unsuccessfully trying to claw from his eyes with his fingers. As the Indian half turned, unsure where his adversary was standing, Anello jumped onto the Choctaw's back, put his left arm tight around the neck, and drove his knife hard in between the Indian's ribs.

Releasing the dead Choctaw, Anello leapt up onto the back of the now spare pony. Grabbing the rope halter, he kicked in his heels to move the animal away, but the second Choctaw, lance pointing ahead of him, was riding straight for him. Aware that there was no way of avoiding the lance, Anello braced himself for having it rip through his body.

But the Choctaw toppled off the back of his pony before Anello caught the crackle of rifle fire. A detail of Confederate soldiers was heading his way at speed, the fact that they were still firing evidence enough to reveal that they had saved him from the Choctaw by accident. They were really after him.

Filled with relief at being mounted again, especially glad that it was on a spirited pony, Anello galloped off, confident that he could distance himself from the pursuing Confederates.

A quarter of an hour later, in the knowledge that he was well out of range of Confederate rifles, Anello eased his pace. He had to rely on this pony to get him close to General Lee's headquarters. Captain Witsell had been killed by the Osages, he had slain Peck. Now there were just the lieutenants, Woodward, Mallory, Mack and Siegle to go. When Silver Moon had been fully avenged, then Captain August Anello could return to the Union army and fight in the war.

Four

Sprawling and ugly, it was a boisterous town. The residents, visiting cowboys, farmers and drovers were vastly outnumbered by Confederate soldiers who caroused in the mindless way of men destined for the battlefields. At the centre of the town's night-life was Warwick DeSantis' saloon. A big place for big men, it was claimed to have the longest bar in the world. This boast was most probably open to challenge, but there was a magnificence in the horseshoe-shaped mahogany bar that measured a curved length of six hundred and fifty feet. Paintings of classical nudes adorned the walls, while a real novelty was an eight-piece ladies' orchestra that occupied a concert stage at the far end of the main floor. A rule that no women were allowed in the bar area was rigidly enforced. Some said this helped keep the place peaceful, while others claimed it caused frustration that led to arguments, fist-fights and gun-fights. Though they found the saloon rough and tough, drinkers appreciated DeSantis' prices; a sixteen-

Epitaph of Vengeance

ounce schooner of beer for a nickel, and two shots of whiskey for a quarter. At these sorts of prices a cowboy could wash the discomfort of the trail from his memory, and a soldier could get so drunk that the prospect of combat lost at least some of its dread.

The saloon had three entry-ways, and August Anello chose the main one, which had swinging doors and led off the main street. Two days ago he had traded in his Indian pony. He gave it and money on top to a nester in exchange for a bay gelding that was a jughead but didn't attract attention coming into town the way the Choctaw pony would have done.

Making his way to the bar he ordered a drink and looked around him. Grey-uniformed Confederates were everywhere, the majority enlisted men, but there was a sprinkling of officers, too. Most of them were the worse for drink, but Anello recognized that he had to be patient. To ask even the most innocuous of questions this close to General Lee's headquarters would arouse suspicion. He watched two lieutenants, both of them youngish, talking in the too serious manner that alcohol induces. Could either or both of them be the men he sought? Doubting that this was so, he accepted that the field of search had widened. Finding Lieutenant Peck so easily had been a stroke of luck too fantastic to be repeated.

The female orchestra finished playing 'All Quiet along the Potomac', and, after a pause, coaxed the haunting strains of 'Lorena' from their instruments. The vast bar went quiet as men listened to the love song that was said to have seduced homesick Confederate soldiers into deserting.

Finding the tune and the atmosphere it created to be strangely moving, Anello thought sadly of Silver Moon. Then Sister Joseph came into his mind, saintly as a nun but compelling as a woman. He found himself comparing Sister Joseph with Loossantech. He hadn't ever given Silver Moon's sister much thought, but now he saw her as something of an Indian equivalent to the nun.

This was dangerously woolly thinking for a man on a mission of death, and Anello had decided to bring it to an end when a voice spoke close by to snap him back to alertness.

'The song does have a special quality, don't you think?'

The speaker was a man whose smart clothes, which included a brightly flowered silken vest, and groomed appearance isolated him in this palace of ruffians. He had a strong face and a light in his eyes that warned it would be foolish to even consider mocking his foppish appearance.

Realizing that it was he who had been addressed, Anello shrugged. 'I'm not sure that I've heard it before.'

'Mmmm, really,' the well-dressed man murmured softly and thoughtfully. Then he smiled and extended his right hand. 'Forgive me, it was most impolite not to introduce myself. Warwick DeSantis. I have the good fortune, or misfortune, depending on my mood, to be the proprietor of this establishment.'

'August Anello,' Anello shook hands, finding it easy to drop the 'Captain' now.

'Look at them, all spellbound by a simple tune,' an incredulous DeSantis remarked as he scanned the bar. 'I have heard that "Lorena" has so demoralized the Confederate army that General John Hunt Morgan has ordered his officers to kill the man who wrote it.'

'Do you believe that?' Anello enquired, although he lacked real interest in this odd conversation.

The question made DeSantis laugh. 'I listen to everything but believe nothing, Anello. For instance, it doesn't do for a man to enquire into the business of another man, but if you were to tell me that you are here in town just by chance, then I most certainly wouldn't believe you.'

Suspicions aroused, made ill at ease, Anello retorted, 'Just as I wouldn't believe you singled me out in this bar for no reason.'

No one was to be trusted in this war. There were spies and double-spies on both sides. Anello couldn't possibly see any way that he could have been expected to arrive here, but DeSantis appeared to know something.

'You are right, of course, I purposely picked you out,' DeSantis admitted.

'Why, I have to be a stranger to you?'

'Indeed you are,' DeSantis smiled at him. 'I had never laid eyes on you until you walked in that door, and when you spoke your name it was the first time I had ever heard it.'

This was reassuring for Anello, who believed the saloon owner because there was no way what he was saying could be anything but the truth. He asked, 'Then why did you approach me, DeSantis?'

'Because there is something I want done, and you're the only man here who looks like he could do it.'

'I'm not a hired gun,' Anello warned the saloon owner.

Signalling the bartender, who passed him a full bottle of whiskey and two glasses, DeSantis said, 'I didn't see you as one. Join me for a drink out back, and I'll explain.'

The female orchestra had left the stage. A young man at the piano was singing:

My Mary Ann's a teacher
In a great big public school

Following DeSantis into an ornately furnished room at the rear of the saloon, Anello sank deeply into the comfortable chair that was offered to him. DeSantis sat at a table, pouring two drinks. As he did so he pushed a newspaper toward Anello, indicating a particular story by tapping on it with a forefinger.

Taking what proved to be a local paper, Anello read a short column that said Kansas Withers, a girl from a local brothel who had been found guilty of stabbing a client to death, was to be hanged in town at noon the next day.

Epitaph of Vengeance 73

'So?' he asked, pushing the newspaper back in DeSantis' direction.

Passing him a full glass, DeSantis told him, 'That girl means a lot to me, Anello. We hit town together a couple of years back and I owe her just about everything, including this place. I can't let them hang her.'

'You don't expect me to walk out on the main street at noon and stop them?' Anello, puzzled, took a sip of his drink.

Shaking his head, smiling at such a ridiculous suggestion, DeSantis replied, 'No, it's much easier than that. Kansas took off after killing that guy. She was tried in her absence. They're bringing her in from Wesselton by stage tomorrow morning.'

'I don't hold up stagecoaches, either,' Anello said as he drained his glass to show that he considered the meeting to have ended.

DeSantis saw things differently and refilled Anello's glass, saying, 'A hold-up would be unnecessary. If you rode to Wesselton tonight you could get on the stage in the morning. Whoever's guarding Kansas won't be expecting trouble. When you reach Bitterroot Creek you pull a gun on the escort, and I'll have someone waiting there to take Kansas Withers off your hands.'

'This is all a bit one-sided, DeSantis,' Anello objected. 'Just supposing I do what you ask, what's in it for me?'

'I'll help you with what you've come here for.'

'How do you know why I'm here?' Anello questioned.

'I don't,' DeSantis answered, 'but you are obviously here for a reason, and I know this town inside out, therefore I can be of assistance to you.'

Interested now, but wary, Anello enquired, 'Where do your sympathies lie, DeSantis, North or South?'

'With whoever has money to spend in my establishment,' DeSantis gave a carefree smile. 'I'm just a businessman, pure and simple. Now, try me with what you want.'

'Confederate officers, all lieutenants,' Anello said. 'Their names are Woodward, Mallory, Mack and Siegle.'

Head bowed in brief thought, DeSantis then said, 'Gardiner Woodward and Alex Mack I know well. But I know nothing of the others you name.'

'I'm happy with two out of four right now,' Anello assented.

'What do I have to do?' DeSantis asked.

'Just point them out to me, DeSantis.'

'I'll sure do that,' the saloon owner grinned, adding meaningfully, 'Right after you get back from helping Kansas.'

'I'm pleased to do business with you, DeSantis,' Anello said, standing up to leave.

'I won't let you down, and I know it will be the same with you,' DeSantis spoke gravely. 'I guess I don't have feelings about much other than money, but Kansas Withers is right special to me.'

Kansas Withers was not what Anello had expected. Auburn-haired and petite, with a face that held character rather than beauty, she was quietly spoken and self-confident. Everything had gone ridiculously easily. As DeSantis had instructed, Anello had left his horse at the livery in Wesselton to be brought to Bitterroot Creek for him by the people who would be collecting the girl. Her escort on the stage had been a feeble father and son with no dedication to their job. Both had meekly surrendered the girl to Anello. Neither the driver of the coach, nor its one other passenger, an elderly rancher, wanted to interfere. The stage was stopped just long enough for the girl and Anello to get off, then it had gone on its way.

Now the two of them sat together, invisibly separated by the awkwardness that afflicts strangers, on a fallen log beside the creek. Although impatient to get back and have the two Confederate officers identified for him, Anello would keep his part of the bargain by delivering the girl to the people DeSantis was sending. Kansas Withers showed absolutely no reaction to having been saved from the hangman. A pensive expression on her face, she stared at the few ripples on the surface of water that was all but static.

'I take it this is Warwick DeSantis' doing,' she remarked absently.

'He wanted you saved,' Anello agreed.

'More's the pity,' the girl said unhappily. 'I really believed that from today I would be free of that man.'

Anello was shocked. DeSantis had given him the impression that Kansas and himself were long-term lovers as well as some kind of business partners, yet she seemed filled with resentment toward the saloon owner.

'Are you saying that you wanted to die?' Anello couldn't really credit that he was asking such a question of so young a girl.

'That's it exactly,' she morosely replied, leaning to pluck a wild rose from a nearby bush, twirling the flower in her fingers, studying it as she went on. 'I was ready to welcome the noose, providing my skirts were tied down to give me a dignity in death that I never had in life.'

She said this so bitterly that Anello didn't doubt that she was telling the truth. He could only say, 'I don't understand.'

'I'm twenty-five years old, mister,' she said, eyes still on the rose. Then she raised her head to study him before commenting, 'You don't look to me like a man who ever had much call for working girls.'

'Can't say that I have.'

She welcomed this confirmation with a nod. 'I thought not. The way it is, mister, in a year or so I'll have a laudanum habit, then there'll be venereal disease and several botched abortions. I'll never make it to thirty.'

'But you'll be out of it now,' Anello told her. 'DeSantis said that these people coming to pick you up will be taking you home to Wichita.'

With a harsh cackle of a laugh, Kansas said flatly, 'The only place Dorita Mustache will take me to is the nearest bordello that she runs.'

It was clear to Anello now. DeSantis had duped

him. The only interest the saloon owner had in rescuing Kansas Withers was to have her continue earning money for him. For the first time since making his agreement with DeSantis, Anello saw it as unlikely that he would ever be shown Woodward and Mack by the saloon owner.

'Dorita Mustache?' Anello queried.

Kansas gave him a scornful look. 'You work for Warwick DeSantis, mister, so you know Dorita.'

'I don't work for DeSantis,' he put her right. 'I did this for him and he promised me something in return.'

'I wouldn't put much store in his promises,' Kansas warned him, adding, 'As for Dorita Mustache, you'll know her when you see her. She's got hair on her top lip that you can spot from a mile away.'

'I didn't realize things were how you say they are,' Anello said.

'They're a whole lot worse than I said,' she told him. Standing to face a disconcerted Anello, the girl raised the bottoms of her coat and shirt. Using a thumb, she pulled down her skirts to reveal the soft, white skin of her bare midriff. An inch or two to the right of her navel was an ugly wound. It was a wide, deep pit in her abdomen that her trimly attractive figure made all the more distressing to look at. 'I did that a year or two back, mister. I tried to find a way out by putting a .36 calibre Smith and Wesson against my own belly and pulling the trigger. A sawbones by the name of Doc Hallett saved me. I haven't ever forgiven him.'

Able to with difficulty grasp how life could be horrendous enough for a girl to do that to herself, Anello numbly watched Kansas cover herself up, tucking her shirt inside her skirts. She looked keenly at him.

'Self-pity didn't make me show you that, mister,' she explained. 'I just wanted you to know that you did me no favours when you saved me from the hangman!'

'Maybe so, but I wouldn't want you dead,' Anello said truthfully.

'Do you mean that?' she asked, wanting to believe him but influenced by a profound mistrust accumulated over a hard lifetime.

'I always mean what I say,' Anello assured her.

With a shrug, she asked, 'Why would it matter to you whether I lived or died?'

'Perhaps the day will come when I will answer that question for you,' he said, after a few moments' hesitation.

Hope and need flashed briefly across her face, softening it so that a special loveliness showed through. But it was all too transient for Anello, and her habitual cynicism returned as she told him, 'I endure too many nightmares to bother with daydreaming, mister.'

'My name's August, August Anello.'

Accepting this with a nod, she remarked, 'It sounds nice, but what's in a name. I've been called Kansas for so long that I've just about forgotten my given name. Anyway, all that don't matter. What was

Warwick DeSantis supposed to be going to do for you, August?'

'He was going to identify two Confederate officers I'm after.'

'What's their names?'

'Lieutenants Woodward and Mack. Do you know them, Kansas?'

'I know them,' she answered, then made a query. 'Do you intend to kill them?'

Anello was unsure how to reply. Already having dismissed DeSantis as being any help to him in the future, he would welcome Kansas Withers pointing the two Confederates out to him. To admit that he was going to kill them would probably alienate her; but he didn't want to tell her a lie.

'They killed someone I was very close to,' he told her cautiously.

'A woman?'

'Yes,' he replied, slightly amused by her curiosity, despite the seriousness of the circumstances. 'An Indian girl.'

'I didn't have you down as a squaw man,' Kansas said teasingly, 'but you can rely on me to help you. First we've got to deal with them two.'

Looking in the direction to which Kansas had gestured with a nod of her head, Anello saw two riders come over a knoll and continue toward them. One was a man, tall in the saddle, the other a woman, squat and with an uncomfortable look to the way she sat her horse. They trailed two saddled horses, the spotted rump of one distinguishing it as an

Appaloosa, the second a piebald.

'That's Nige Clayton, he's really mean, and the ugly cow is Dorita Mustache,' Kansas critically identified the riders.

Easing his .45 a little way up out of its holster, then dropping it back, satisfied with the test, he assured his companion, 'I'll take care of you.'

'That won't be necessary, August,' she said, adding a caution, 'Their orders will be to take me to one of Dorita's places. DeSantis doesn't need you any more, so it's you that's in danger.'

'Howdy,' Clayton said as he and the woman reined up.

Built in that gangling, loose-limbed manner which Anello knew was likely to mean excellent reflexes and a fast speed of movement, Nige Clayton, long-necked and beak-nosed, looked every bit as mean as Kansas had warned he was. The woman had on a floppy-brimmed hat that partially concealed her plain, round face, but Anello could see the dark, downy layer on her upper lip.

'Howdy,' Anello returned the greeting, touching the brim of his stetson respectfully to the woman, who did nothing but sit absolutely still, staring at him, her hands on the saddle horn in front of her, but covered by the poncho she had on.

Pulling the Appaloosa forward, Clayton spoke conversationally. 'This here bronc's for you, pardner. He's got plenty of bottom. . . .'

'Watch him, August,' Kansas said in an insistent whisper.

Anello was not sure then or afterwards, whether it was the warning from Kansas or his own self-preservation instinct that had him spring into action. Using the pretence of bringing up the spare horse to turn his right side away from Anello, and keeping him occupied by talking, Clayton was drawing his gun when Anello drew and fired his Colt.

The impact of the slug lifted Clayton sideways out of the saddle. As he went off his horse, one foot caught in the stirrup. Panicked by the noise of the shot and the sudden, uneven weight of Clayton dragging on it, the horse leapt about. One of its hoofs smashed into the face of an already dead Clayton, mashing the flesh and bones of the corpse, freeing the foot from the stirrup in the process. The horse settled down, while the Appaloosa and the piebald remained calm and motionless. Anello let his gun slide back into its holster.

Breaking the silence that settled as the echoes of Anello's shot died away, Dorita Mustache spoke in a grating voice that fitted her appearance. 'I'm holding a Derringer under this poncho, Anello, and it's pointed right at your heart. Don't get to thinking it's just powder and ball. It's packing a .41 calibre cartridge.'

'Gun her down, August,' Kansas, standing close to his right side, urged.

'I can't shoot a woman,' Anello confessed, the pleased look that came over Dorita's hairy face making him feel even worse about the situation.

'I can!'

As he heard Kansas say those two words, so did Anello feel her take his gun from his holster with her left hand. She tossed the heavy Colt with ease to her right hand, firing all in one rapid, deft movement.

Although it seemed Dorita Mustache had fired her Derringer simultaneously, she must have been a fraction of a second behind Kansas. The slug from the Derringer passed between Anello's left arm and his chest, plucking at his clothing as it went. He saw the squat body of the woman slump forward, one arm going round the neck of her horse, the other hanging loosely.

Keeping Anello's Colt, holding it steadily in her right hand, Kansas walked up to tug on the wrist of the arm that held Dorita Mustache on her horse. The heavy body toppled sideways to land face down. Walking over, keeping the fallen body covered with the .45, Kansas got a toe under the woman's shoulder and turned her onto her back.

'Dead!' Kansas declared with satisfaction, walking back to Anello. Replacing his gun in its holster, she said, 'Well, August, we got horses now, so let's go find those Confederates you're after.'

Astonished by what she had done, he stood still for a moment, looking at her. This worried her. Having got hold of the reins of the piebald, she asked worriedly, 'You having doubts about teaming up with a whore, August?'

Shaking his head, he looked down at the dead Dorita and commented wryly, 'I guess you'll be real handy to have along.'

Epitaph of Vengeance 83

'I have my uses,' she grinned at him, mounting up as he went to the Appaloosa. They were about to ride away when she brought her horse in front of his to stop him from moving ahead. Wearing a frown, she asked, 'Is Warwick DeSantis on your list with the Confederates now?'

'Do you want him to be, Kansas?'

Shaking her head, causing long, auburn ringlets to dance, she answered, 'No. I want to go into that town, help you do what you want to do, then get out. DeSantis is bad medicine, August. He's got that town tied up, and to go against him would be dangerous.'

'He's not important,' he told her.

'Good. Then let's be on our way.'

'What will you do, afterwards, Kansas?' Anello enquired as they rode side by side. 'You can't go back to your old work, not around here, anyway, now that you blew a hole in that fat woman.'

'I'm getting right out of it,' Kansas said decidedly.

They had left the creek, skirting some willows, serenaded by birds singing a welcome to approaching twilight. Anello remarked, 'It isn't easy for a woman to get by alone.'

'I could always ride with you,' Kansas hopefully suggested.

'That won't be possible,' he told her gently.

'My mistake,' she said bitterly. 'I should have known you'd be choosy. I suppose that Indian girl's spirit is still with you.'

Reining up, wanting to make himself clear, he waited until Kansas had stopped beside him. 'I'll never forget Silver Moon, but it's not that. I'm a captain in the Union army, Kansas, and I've got to get back to my unit when I've taken care of the men who killed her.'

'A Yankee officer,' Kansas gave a whistle of surprise through her teeth. 'You sure know how to keep a girl guessing, August.'

Spurring her horse, she rode off. When he caught up with her he said, 'You help me get these fellows, Kansas, and I'll make sure that you have somewhere safe and comfortable to stay.'

'Then one day you'll come back for me?' she asked with heavy sarcasm.

'Like I said before, that's another question I might be able to answer one day, Kansas.'

Looking at him sadly, she murmured, 'I've heard all the questions, August, but I'm resigned to never getting one answer.'

They rode on into a new night then, both staying silent because they found they had nothing to say to each other.

Five

Rifle bullets clipped the sagebrush close to the prone figures of Kansas Withers and August Anello. Other slugs spattered against the low rocky grade behind which they had taken cover. Some of the bullets became dangerous for a second time by glancing off angled surfaces to spin around their heads with a whining, whistling sound. A torrid sun heated their backs in a way that surpassed discomfort to become painful. Those firing at them had the complete upper hand, able to move in and finish them off, or bide their time until surrender was the only option. Anello knew now that he had made a bad mistake in having the girl and himself bed down for the night, delaying their return to town. High in the hills, they had lit no fire, eating cold the tinned meat that Anello carried in his saddle-bags. Its taste was unpleasant enough to justify the nickname of 'embalmed beef' given it by Union soldiers. Their humble meal had been enhanced by clear, refreshing water from a stream. In the morning they had dallied, enjoying the relaxing warmth of an early sun yet to gain its full power. Both had considered it would be an advantage to keep DeSantis guessing for a time.

But he must have learned what had happened at Bitterroot Creek and had called on the Confederate army for help. Despite DeSantis having claimed total neutrality when in conversation with Anello, Kansas said that the man who owned the saloon and most of the town had strong Southern sympathies. The fact that the two of them were now surrounded and pinned down by Confederate soldiers confirmed that DeSantis had reported Anello's search for the two lieutenants.

Sizing up the situation, Anello had to quickly reach out an arm to pin Kansas down as a dangerously close bullet spat dirt and sand into her eyes and she automatically jerked up. He held her safely flat to the ground until she had blinked away the worst of the soreness. Escape to the north, south or east was impossible. The only trail not cut off was the one going west into town. They wouldn't be expected to take it, and if they did there was sure to be a reception committee awaiting them.

Having used his rifle to return fire, Anello now rammed shells into the hot weapon as Kansas unnecessarily told him, 'We'll never be able to hold out here until nightfall.'

'We've only one chance,' he told her, 'and it's a real risky one.'

'Whatever, it'll be better than lying here,' she said,

Epitaph of Vengeance

her coolness impressing him. 'You decide what to do, and I'll do it.'

'You were ready to die yesterday,' he reminded her jokingly.

'That was before I'd met you,' she replied, and Anello was a little shaken to recognize that she wasn't joking.

Firing three shots, not in the hope of hitting one of the well-concealed soldiers, but to reduce their fire by forcing them to keep their heads down, Anello instructed. 'You stay here while I try to make it back to the horses. When I get to the rim of the wash I'll open up with the rifle to give you a chance to run for it.'

'You'll never make....' Kansas began, but Anello was already sliding away from her on his stomach.

He drew a hail of lead as he crawled along, propelling himself by grasping at the sagebrush. Yet he ran up to reach the lip of the draw unscathed. A glance told him that the pair of horses were still where Kansas and himself had hitched them when first ambushed. Dropping to lie with his head and shoulders up over the rim, he blasted away with his rifle.

Taking that as her signal, Kansas gamely crawled through the brush then came his way at a crouching run. As she came tumbling over the lip of the draw, Anello, still firing, witnessed what had to be the strangest sight of his life. A Confederate bullet neatly sliced off one of Kansas' long, auburn ringlets. The coil of hair hung in the air for a split second, then hit the ground the same time as she did. An anxious Anello saw that an ear against which the curl had lain was bleeding profusely. With no time to check, he guessed that this was no more than a nick.

She must be aware that she had been less than an inch from death, but she crouched below the ridge, looking to him for the next order.

'Mount up, Kansas, and ride!' he shouted while still firing.

'Toward town?' she queried.

'There's no other way,' he called back, accepting that it was hopeless to go in that direction, but feeling that he would be able to think of something once clear of this incessant gunfire.

She ran, and had one foot in a stirrup, swinging up onto the back of the piebald as he vaulted over the rear end of the Appaloosa to land in the saddle and spur the horse away. Bullets were flying round them. Anello, though not anticipating any organized or prolonged pursuit, with the Confederates behind them fully aware that they were riding into the Confederates up ahead in town, was worried by the horse Kansas was riding being unable to keep up with his mount.

Then a bullet touched his boot, taking away leather and skin so that he could feel blood trickling warm and stickily down around his foot. Another bullet raked the piebald's flank, sending it plunging through the sagebrush at a breakneck speed.

By spurring his horse hard, Anello managed to reach Kansas' side. Now unlikely to be followed, and with Kansas' horse slowing as the initial sting from the bullet that had carved a bloody groove along its flank faded, they were some three miles from town. If they left the trail a couple of miles ahead, they could explore the perimeter of the town for a possible undetected entry between buildings. But success was unlikely, for there were bound to be regular Confederate patrols circling the settlement.

They halted to give their mounts a short breather. Kansas, her right shoulder soaked with blood, but with her ear no longer bleeding because it had congealed, looked at him quizzically. Too intelligent to expect him to have a solution to their dire problem, she couldn't stop herself from hoping. There was a dull ache in his own leg, but Anello guessed that had stopped bleeding, too.

She was about to ask a question when Anello raised a hand to silence her. His acute hearing had picked up the jingle of a bridle chain behind them. It had been a fleeting sound, but enough to have him silently urge her to bring the piebald off the trail.

Ten yards back, concealed behind a screen of cottonwoods and willows, they anxiously waited. Now they could both hear the steady, plodding hoofbeats of walking horses. Willing their own mounts not to make any noise, they wondered if the Confederates who'd had them pinned down had caught up with them. There hadn't been time for that, so they assumed that they were unlucky enough to have come across a military detail searching for them.

Five riders, abreast across the trail, came into view.

Wearing dust-covered blue uniforms of the Union army, they were dirty, unshaven and heavily armed, but so relaxed that they were conversing loudly.

At first, believing the five to be Union soldiers totally oblivious to the fact that Confederate soldiers had the road ahead blocked, Anello faced a dilemma. Unable to let men of his own army ride on to their almost certain deaths, he couldn't risk revealing Kansas and himself. Then his crucial problem solved itself as the riders drew nearer. They were speaking English, but Anello was able to detect at least three foreign accents. One was deep, angry-sounding German, another lilting Irish, while the third was the peculiarly distinctive Swedish.

Putting the accents together with the unkempt appearances had Anello identify the men as 'bounty jumpers'. They were opportunists, and there were many of them, who joined the Union army to collect the enlistment bonus, then deserted to sign on elsewhere for another bonus. The bounties paid were large; consequently, these men would be desperate because they would be shot if captured.

As a plan came to Anello, so did the build-up of tension swiftly subside in him. Not wanting to speak to Kansas for fear of his voice carrying, he gave her a smile that he hoped said all would be well.

When the riders had passed out of earshot, he moved the Appaloosa closer to her horse, to say, 'They're deserters, Kansas. If we ride to town behind them, staying close, they are bound to run into the Confederates waiting for us. Those five will have no

Epitaph of Vengeance

choice but to fight to the death.'

'And in the confusion,' Kansas caught on rapidly, 'we should be able to slip into town.'

'You've got it, Kansas! If we make it, can you find us somewhere to hide out?' Anello enquired.

She gave his question thought as she controlled the piebald as it shied away from some patches of cholla. The horse had begun to suffer from the bullet wound now, behaving skittishly and displaying a worrying lameness. Whatever was to happen up ahead, Anello feared that the piebald might well let them down.

'Bel Kellaway will help us,' Kansas said at last, with enough conviction to satisfy Anello. 'She hates Warwick DeSantis every bit as much as the rest of us.'

Checking ahead to determine they were keeping the right distance behind the bounty jumpers, he asked. 'One of the girls?'

'Bel's a widow-woman, she runs the Women's Christian Temperance Union in town,' Kansas turned in her saddle to inform him with a rueful grin.

Thinking at first that she was having fun with him, Anello then realized that Kansas was serious. He commented, 'You sure got me beat with that one, Kansas.'

'Bel's a good sort,' she said with a little laugh. 'She's always on that she wants to save me, so now's her chance.'

'Probably this is not the way she meant,' Anello suggested.

'We can rely on Bel for anything. Like I said, she's a good sort,' Kansas assured him, then stayed quiet as Anello signalled for her to do so.

They slowed before reaching the peak of a rise. They could see the five riders now, ahead where the trail was narrowing. The men were riding down a grey slope that was dotted with junipers. Each side of the trail was strewn with hundreds of boulders, great and small, that had tumbled down in past ages from rocky reefs that thrust upward on either side.

This had to be where the Confederates were waiting. They proved this to be so by firing too soon. Not hitting any of the five bounty jumpers, the Confederates' mistake gave them the chance to dismount and take cover among the rocks. They soon proved that the Union army had lost a group of proficient fighting men when they'd deserted. As four Confederate soldiers rose up from behind rocks, rifles to shoulders, three of them died instantly from the deadly accurate fire of the renegade Unionists, the dying screams of one harrowing as they bounced back and forth off the rocks.

With no time to estimate the size of the force they faced, the bounty jumpers took the fight to the Confederates. Moving through the rocks, firing as they went, they swiftly brought down two more of the enemy. One of the Unionists, a huge, red-bearded fellow, was clambering over a boulder when a Confederate rifle ball went into his back at an angle. Like a giant, clothed frog attempting a leap, he lay atop the rock, alternately bending his knees and stretching his legs, while his blood leaked copiously, running down to paint wide red stripes on the boulder.

The big man's legs finally stilled. He died, as the Confederates, who had been behind boulders on both sides of the trail, panicked. Those to the right of the observing Kansas and Anello came out of hiding to run across the flat in an attempt at joining their comrades on the opposite side. Eight of them tried, only three made it. The withering fire of the four remaining bounty jumpers brought down the other five.

'Pull back!'

As the Confederate order was shouted, with the four remaining Unionists moving relentlessly forward behind their own rapid fire, daylight was failing. Assessing the fight, Anello concluded that it would soon end with a complete rout of the Confederate force, despite their obvious superiority in numbers. It was his guess that they were raw recruits facing fire in anger for the first time, whereas the Union deserters were obviously veteran fighters.

It was time for Kansas and himself to make a move, and he led her off to the right, moving on horseback to the rocks abandoned by the Southern soldiers. Anticipating that they would have to dismount and lead their horses between the large boulders, Anello discovered a rough, twisting bridleway of sorts meandering between the boulders and the sharp rise of the reef.

With the fight still continuing spasmodically over

to their left, they moved past it undetected. Reaching the outskirts of the town with darkness settling around them, they had to pull in between two buildings as hoofbeats pounded behind them and the raggedy remains of the Confederate detail went by.

The way was clear for Kansas and Anello then, as the deserters would have learned not to continue into a town obviously held by the Confederates.

'It's easy enough to ride in,' Anello remarked. then went on to predict, 'but I reckon as how we'll be lucky to ride out.'

This was to be assumed because the Confederates would know that they had slipped past them, and wouldn't be able to relax until they were sure that Anello was no longer a threat to their officers. They most probably believed that Anello was under Union orders as a solitary assassin working behind their lines.

Yet when they reached the main street it was strangely quiet. The saloon of Warwick DeSantis was open and doing business, but there was only a sprinkling of Confederate soldiers among the civilians on the street. When they had negotiated dark back alleyways to leave their horses and enter a house through a rear door, they learned what had brought the change to the town.

After welcoming both Kansas and Anello, Bel Kellaway, cheeks cherry-red and bright blue eyes glistening from the glare of an oil-lamp and Christian zeal, explained the lack of Confederate soldiers in town. 'I hear that the lot of them are moving out in the morning, heading north, so it's said. I suppose most of them are in camp tonight, preparing to leave.'

Anello felt Kansas' anxious gaze. She recognized that this severely limited the time he had to get Woodward and Mack. There was also the very real possibility that both of those officers would be confined to camp that evening. What the girl didn't know was the quandary Anello had been put in by news of the Confederate army moving north. Intelligence gained before leaving Humboldt had him certain General Robert E. Lee's Army of Northern Virginia, numbering seventy thousand men with J.E.B. Stuart's cavalry detached, was taking the war into Union territory. In addition to having a discouraging effect on Union troops, it was a bold move that was likely to have the Confederacy recognized across the world.

At a stroke, Anello's personal vendetta had been relegated to a poor second place in his priorities. It was now vital that he rejoined his outfit before the battles commenced. Though grateful to the widow Kellaway for the information regarding the Confederates, Kansas and himself would not be requiring her hospitality. They would be leaving town again that night.

Telling Kansas this when they were alone, although the ghost of Silver Moon seemed to be with him, he added, 'With your help I'll give finding Woodward and Mack just one more try before we leave.'

'What would you have me do, August?' she willingly enquired.

'Come with me to the door of DeSantis' saloon and look in to see if either or both of them are inside.'

With a vehement shake of her head, Kansas replied, 'No! You can't walk into that place alone. There'll be Confederates there ready to support their officers, and DeSantis has his gunmen there, alert for any trouble. You wouldn't live for one minute after going in through the door, August.'

'I can take care of myself,' he said assuringly, and after a further show of reluctance, she agreed to go with him, although she repeated her worries about him over and over again.

Leaving the horses hitched at the rear of Bel Kellaway's home, Anello decided to put his rifle inside and collect it later when they took their leave of the widow. But Kansas saw it differently.

'We'll say goodbye to you now, Bel,' she said, cuddling the widow to her, 'but we'll be back before too much time has passed.'

'I'll look forward to that,' the widow blinked a few tears away, 'and to seeing you again, August. May God go with both of you.'

'Your rifle,' Kansas said to August, picking up the weapon as they went out.

Carrying it would be a hindrance to him in what he had to do, and he told Kansas, 'It'll get in my way, leave it here.'

'I'll carry it for you,' she said firmly, tucking it

under her arm.

The rifle was still there later, the weight of it having her stand lopsidedly when they were cautiously peering over the double doors into Warwick DeSantis' saloon.

There was a fair-sized crowd inside, mostly civilians, but several men in grey uniforms were playing a game of monte run by a lieutenant. Kansas spoke urgently into Anello's ear. 'The soldier running the game, that is Alexander Mack.'

Anello peered through the flickering changing of light and shadow cast by kerosene lamps. The lieutenant was young, small and with a boyish face. He didn't look capable of the assault on and murder of Silver Moon, but Anello had long ago learned that what went on in a man's head didn't necessarily show on his face. Kansas gave a little tug on his sleeve.

'Woodward,' she said. 'The man with the long hair on Mack's right is Lieutenant Woodward.'

With matted hair falling to his shoulders, Gardiner Woodward looked capable of anything, even the heinous crime committed against the Indian girl. It could have been the blackness of the lieutenant's hair that made his face a deathly white in contrast, Anello couldn't be sure.

'You stay outside, move well away from the door,' Anello, ready to enter the saloon, instructed her.

Hearing but not acknowledging Kansas' plea that he take care, Anello pushed the doors open and went in. Pausing, he scanned behind and in front of the long bar for sight of Warwick DeSantis. If the saloon owner was present he would recognize Anello and have him shot down. Relieved that there was no sign of DeSantis, assuming that he was in the back room, Anello walked casually towards where the game was being played. On his way he placed three of the saloon's gunmen standing at intervals along the bar, another was lounging but alert beside the stage on which the female orchestra was playing, while a fourth stood with his back against the wall about fifteen feet from the game of monte.

'Looking for a game, cowboy?' Mack asked Anello as he walked up. He was more boyish than ever up close, his face almost angelic, which, in Anello's experience, often indicated a killer's mind.

'I ain't rightly sure,' Anello drawled.

'Scared you might lose your payroll, Texas?' the longhaired Woodward asked with a grin that put stained and crooked teeth on show.

The verbal exchange interested the other players, but no one else around seemed to notice either Anello or what was going on.

'It ain't that at all,' Anello replied. 'I allow that your little game is just too tame for me.'

'Tame!' Lieutenant Mack snorted indignantly. 'This is a man's game, *amigo*. You ready to put your money where your mouth is?'

'This ain't the sort of game I'm looking for,' Anello explained. 'What I'm looking for is some real fun, like you can have with a young Osage girl.'

Not missing the quick glance the two Confederates shared, Anello saw both men unbutton

Epitaph of Vengeance

the flap of their army-issue holsters, worn waist high on belts outside their uniform coats. In particular he watched Mack, who was the more agitated of the two.

'Take it easy, Alex,' Woodward, worried by his comrade's nervousness, advised.

'Her name was Silver Moon,' Anello said, deliberately putting pressure on Mack.

A tic started to pull at the left side of the boyish Confederate's bow-lipped mouth. Woodward, who remained cool, said something soothing that Anello couldn't decipher and Lieutenant Mack completely ignored.

His fingers grasping the butt of his revolver was the last conscious move Alexander Mack would ever make. Drawing and firing, Anello saw his bullet smash the baby face of the Confederate into a bloody red and purple mess of splintered bone, ripped-apart flesh with the white of shattered teeth showing through grotesquely.

At the sound of the shot the music came to a string-screeching halt, and the women musicians were making subdued little squeals of alarm.

Knowing that Woodward had his gun clear of the holster, but unable to turn in time to beat him to the shot, Anello kicked out at a small table beside him, catching the Confederate officer in the groin. This caused only a slight delay, but it was enough for Anello to shoot Woodward through the heart.

Now the women from the band were screaming wildly. As the second Confederate crashed dead to the floor, lying obliquely to his companion, the house gunmen sprung into action. The one leaning against the wall straightened up and drew his six-gun just as a bullet from Anello tore most of his throat away. The whole scene was clear to Anello. He glimpsed DeSantis coming out of the back room, and was surprised by the sight of Kansas, holding his rifle, step in through a rear door. He was in immediate danger from the gunman at the bar who was nearest to him. The fellow had drawn and dropped to a crouch. As he looked at the muzzle of the gun trained on him, Anello accepted that he could never draw a bead on the man before he fired.

Then a rifle shot boomed like an explosion inside the room. A kerosene lamp hanging high above the bar disintegrated, falling onto the gunman. Letting out a roar of pain, the gunman dropped to roll on the floor, his hair alight and the burning oil spreading down his back to set his clothing on fire.

There was pandemonium then. Hollering out in terror, the man was burning to death, having those around him hesitate about whether to help him or get Anello. Warwick DeSantis was shouting orders, but appeared to be no more than miming because he couldn't be heard in the uproar. Stepping further into the room, the rifle up to her shoulder, Kansas coolly and methodically shot out the five remaining oil-lamps in turn. On impulse, Anello fired at where he had last seen DeSantis. He heard a gasping grunt and the thud of a body hitting the floor.

As the last lamp exploded and its light died away, her voice came to Anello through the dark made deep by its newness.

'To me, August!'

Running, colliding with a man who drew back from him in fear, and crashing against a table with such force that it took him a moment to right himself, Anello felt fresh air coming in the back door. Then Kansas' hand was placed guidingly on his arm and he went out beside her into the night.

'If we walk we won't draw attention to ourselves,' she cautioned as they moved away from the saloon. 'I know a back way to get to Bel's.'

As they went, reaching their horses and mounting up, Kansas asked him, 'Did you get Warwick DeSantis?'

'I'm not sure,' Anello answered.

'Oh, well,' she sighed, 'nothing's perfect.'

'You are,' he said, meaning it because of the way she had helped him, saved him, that night.

Silent for a moment as they slowly rode out of town, she then gave a self-critical chuckle before saying, 'That's no way to describe an out of work whore, August!'

Six

There was frantic activity as Troop D, 6th Kansas Cavalry, prepared to move out. There was a constant pounding of marching feet, sometimes at the double as squads on pressing assignments were hurried along. All that seemed to be keeping a theme of order running through a scene of mass chaos were the incessant, shouted commands of non-commissioned officers. Men on fatigue duty were loading wagons with spiked logs that would be used to protect defensive positions. In anticipation of casualties, rows of two-wheeled, springless ambulance carts were lined up ready to leave. Horses were being harnessed to gun-carriages, while struggling, sweating troopers hitched up caissons and limbers. Members of religious groups wandered around handing pamphlets to any soldiers prepared to take them.

This was a pre-battle time when an army came into its own, almost taking on a grandeur, but Colonel Blueth kept the meeting between Captain Anello

Epitaph of Vengeance 103

and himself informal. Sipping whiskey in the Colonel's tent, Anello was made ill at ease by the temporary removal of rank between them. Capable of maintaining impeccable poise either at military briefings or on social occasions, he discovered this to be disconcertingly halfway between those two things.

Some ten years older than him, Blueth had the haughty aloofness of a man totally dedicated to the army. If his type ever did relax their stiff-backed, disciplined manner, then there was no one around to witness it. Anello had never, would never, be one of them. Although a member of the military and a highly respected officer, he had never sacrificed his individuality as a human being. Right then Anello was thankful for that, for even though Blueth was attempting to act like a brother officer, there was a perturbing coldness to him. Anello had been straight with his immediate superior, saying that he had set aside tracking down Mallory and Siegle until the coming confrontation with the Confederate army was over. The colonel accepted this without comment, much of his mind projected to the battlefields of tomorrow.

Having come to know his commanding officer well, Anello assessed Blueth as a person made sad by an ever-present conflict within himself. A married man with three young children, the colonel was torn between a longing to be home with his wife and family, and a need to make a name for himself as a military commander.

'We are to be part of Major-General George G.

Meade's Army of the Potomac, August,' a proud Blueth revealed as he partly recharged Anello's glass. A mean man, the colonel was prudent with everything but personal courage. Anello could vouch for the latter, as he had been at Blueth's side during many a bloody encounter with a foe.

'A considerable force, sir,' Anello made a comment that was really a probe.

'Close to ninety thousand men, August, close to ninety thousand men.'

That was some army. Impressed, Anello also recognized that whatever had gone before in the war would be nothing compared to what was about to happen. As a soldier who never fooled himself, he realized that he was both excited and apprehensive. A man was a liar if he said that before a battle he didn't give thought to the chances of his own survival. What was occurring now was even more stressful. From the moment the 6th Kansas Cavalry rode out of camp, life would never be the same again for anyone.

Anello considered the future, if the battles to come were to permit him to have one. Grateful to Kansas Withers for the invaluable assistance and support she had given him in his quest, Anello had secured her safety by taking her to the partly completed mission of Sister Joseph. On arriving there, finding himself still drawn to the nun, Anello had been encouraged by a glimpse of what he believed to be jealousy in Sister Joseph on her noticing how close Kansas and he were. Since then he had continually told himself that he had misconstrued the nun's reaction. It was an insult to both Sister Joseph and her faith to consider that she was subject to so base an emotion.

Though she hadn't put her question into words, Kansas had asked with her eyes if he would be coming back for her. Not proud of having avoided making any kind of commitment to the girl, who he knew had a low opinion of herself because of her former profession, Anello had also ridden away without saying a word of farewell to Sister Joseph. Both of those omissions filled him with regret now. Should his life soon end under cannon fire or from a Confederate bullet, he had left loose ends that those remaining behind could never tie. It was an example of what Silver Moon, who liked everything to have a purpose, and wanted a purpose for everything, referred to as 'tangled destiny'. August Anello was better at killing than he was at untangling things.

'That should be enough men to ensure success, sir,' he said.

'There were one hundred and fifty thousand men under General Hooker at Chancellorsville, Captain,' Colonel Blueth reminded him, the bitter memory making him rank-conscious once more, 'and we lost that one, badly. That must not happen again.'

Anello was in tacit agreement. In the high number of casualties in that fight the Confederates had lost Thomas J. 'Stonewall' Jackson, while Anello had lost Lieutenant Alan Bressaw, a man who had been a close friend throughout his army career. Hooker's failure had him replaced by Meade, who was trusted to bring victory to the Union army in the battles to come.

Draining his glass as a prelude to dismissing Anello, Blueth shook the captain's hand, saying, 'It's good to have you back, August. I would not have been confident fighting without you.'

'Thank you, sir,' Anello replied.

Outside the tent Anello could sense a collective tension in the morning air. It was a familiar feeling that would disappear when the first shot was fired. He paused to watch George Milnar repetitively put a squad of supporting infantrymen through loading drill with Springfield rifles. It was a mock procedure, for ammunition was too precious to be wasted in practice. Aware that the sergeant was devoting time to come as close as possible to perfection before combat, Anello studied what progress was being made.

On Milnar's first command the troopers used their teeth to tear open an imaginary paper cartridge containing powder and ball. As the sergeant rapped out his second order, powder was poured down the barrels. Then thumbs pushed in bullets. 'Draw ramrods!' Sergeant Milnar shouted and the troops obeyed, pushing the projectiles down the barrels. With the penultimate order having them pull back the hammers, they finally placed the percussion caps on the nibs beneath the hammers. Had real ammunition been used the rifles would have been ready to fire.

Epitaph of Vengeance 107

On the whole the exercise had a smoothness to it. But the soldiers were untried. There was a world of difference between a parade-ground drill with pretend powder and ball, and the stark, often terrifying reality of loading rifles under heavy fire. Anello knew that Milnar, a veteran like himself, would have misgivings about how his men would handle this procedure when under fire for the first time.

Catching sight of Anello, Milnar ordered his men to stand easy. Coming toward Anello in his usual upright, soldierly style, the sergeant threw up a smart salute. 'May I welcome you back, sir?'

'Thank you, George,' Anello said as he returned the salute.

'Might I ask if your objective was achieved, sir?'

Not welcoming Milnar's rigid military manner because he regarded the sergeant as a friend, Anello would do nothing to discourage it. Milnar was an excellent example for the men to follow. He represented what soldiering was all about, and therefore had to be correct at all times.

'Three of them are dead, Sergeant,' Anello replied.

'And the other two, sir?'

'They'll keep, Sergeant, until we've dealt with this push General Lee is making,' the captain said. 'You've done good work with the men, George. My worry is that I foresee a lot of hand-to-hand combat. Has there been any bayonet practice?'

'I broached the matter to Colonel Blueth, sir, but he was of the opinion that we don't have the time.'

Giving a nod, Anello understood. None of the

men ever seemed prepared to get involved with their triangular-shaped bayonets that were eighteen inches long. Going queasy when contemplating fighting with fixed bayonets, the soldiers preferred to use them as spits for roasting meat, or candle-holders. Colonel Blueth was right. There was perhaps time to fit in some bayonet practice, but getting a trooper to accept his bayonet for its proper use would be a long process.

'Do you want me to teach the men, sir?'

'No, George, like the colonel says, there is no time,' Anello said. 'You're doing a great job as it is.'

'Sir,' Milnar responded, too old a soldier to reveal that Anello's praise had pleased him.

'When were you last on the Osage Reserve, George?' Anello tried to appear casual as he made the enquiry.

'About a week ago, sir,' Milnar replied. 'Loossantech is safe and well, sir, but still grieves for her sister, of course.'

'I didn't ask that, Sergeant,' Anello said, suppressing a grin at the astute Milnar's unusual forwardness. 'I enquired because it is essential to have the Osage tribesmen remain loyal to the Union.'

His involvement with Silver Moon had brought Anello close to the Osage. He felt sorry for the Indians, who were disillusioned by the white man's broken promises, and confused by a war they had no real understanding of.

Sergeant Milnar spoke without being spoken to, which was something he never did in the presence of

Epitaph of Vengeance

an officer. 'It is my understanding, sir, that the Osage are about to move the village to a point east of the Verdigris River.'

It distressed Anello to learn this, as his sergeant had known it would. Loossantech had been on his mind a lot of late. Although she lacked the shyness that had made her late sister so charming, the older Indian girl was remarkably good-looking, and had a unique, powerful presence. Experiencing a stab of guilt where Silver Moon was concerned, it pained him that the Osage were to move so far away, depriving him of the opportunity to spend at least a little time with the enchanting Loossantech. Never previously having worn his heart on his sleeve, he now found himself thinking almost obsessively about three women, one of them an Indian, the second a prostitute, and the third a nun. Without him choosing it to be that way, life made a habit of becoming complicated for August Anello.

'Carry on, Sergeant,' he said, sending Milnar back to the squad he was training.

Walking off, intending to check on the supplies being loaded, Anello was stopped by a tall, thin civilian dressed poorly but neatly. Without saying a word, the man pressed a pamphlet into Anello's hand, then added a second. Glancing at the titles, Anello read *Why Do You Swear?* and *The Destitution and Wretchedness of a Drunkard.*

His exceptionally bright eyes studying Anello deeply, the man offered, 'If you need to talk to someone before you leave, brother, you will find me somewhere around the camp.'

'Thank you,' Anello replied out of politeness, although he had no intention of taking up the offer. On the rare occasions when he felt it necessary, he had spoken to the Catholic priests who moved among the Osage. Now Sister Joseph seemed to sustain him spiritually, but remotely.

As he watched the colporteur walk away, a figure made eerie by the long, black, threadbare cloak that swept the ground as he moved, Anello became aware of something or someone on the road behind him attracting the attention of a squad of soldiers who were loading supplies.

Turning, he saw an Indian woman approaching. She came along the centre of the road. There was much pride in her upright walk and the way she held her lovely head high. Anello was reminded of a painting he had seen hanging on the wall of Major-General Hooker's office. Depicting an Indian princess it had been entitled *The Beautiful Savage*. Thinking that this was an apt description for the lovely creature heading toward him, Anello suddenly recognized her as Loossantech.

He would have identified her before had he not been convinced that she was many miles away. Smiling, he went to meet her. But her striking face held no smile for him. Neither was it impassive in the way of an Indian. There seemed to be a suppressed anger in her.

'Captain Anello,' she addressed him coldly. 'Are the men who killed my sister now dead?'

The way she asked betrayed that she already knew the answer. Somehow, in the mystical way that information travels over great distances between Indians, she had learned that his task of vengeance had only been half completed.

'Two of the men remain,' he told her. 'But I will track them down. Your sister, your family, and yourself, Loossantech, will be avenged. I promise you that.'

'When?' she enquired harshly, her eyes going past him to where the military preparations were nearing completion. 'Now you are going to fight the war of white men. By forgetting my sister you insult her memory, Captain Anello.'

'I could never forget Silver Moon,' he averred, hurt by her accusation. That hurt was tempered by an overwhelming excitement at being in her presence. There was much he wanted to say to Loossantech, but it would be intimate talk that would probably serve to convince her further that he had abandoned her dead sister.

'Go, fight your war, Captain Anello,' she said, turning on her heel.

'Wait,' he cried, reaching out to catch hold of her hand to prevent her from walking away from him. It was a strong hand with slim fingers together with some magical property that made his whole body tingle at the contact between them. 'There are things I must say to you, Loossantech.'

'I wish no talk with you,' she spoke forcefully. Lifting her free hand she held up two fingers. 'I wait two moons, no longer, Captain Anello. If you have not killed those two men by then, I will track them down and kill them. Then I will come after you, and take your life for not revenging my sister.'

She had stated an impossible time limit. It could well be two moons before they even made contact with the Confederates. Anello wanted to explain that, to impress on her that he would never rest until those who had killed Silver Moon were dead. But she snatched her hand free of his, gave him a look of sheer contempt, and walked off in her proud way.

That contemptuous look kept Anello awake that night, and it even haunted his dreams during the short periods of sleep he managed to get. In the morning, with the blue-uniformed might of the Union army all around him, although he desperately wanted to he could not remember the beautiful face of Loossantech without the look she had given him destroying his memory of her.

They rode out soon after dawn, and there was something stirring about it. A humble, solitary musician, a trooper playing a harmonica, the reins of his horse tucked under an arm, played 'John Brown's Body', while the soldiers sang, somewhat discordantly but lustily.

'We are off to war,' Colonel Blueth said in so soft a voice that Anello, who rode beside his commanding officer, couldn't tell whether the colonel was expressing rejoicing or regret.

Then Anello didn't care which it was. Loossantech, looking exactly as she had when taking her acrimonious leave of him, came back into his head to drive out all other thoughts.

Seven

Anello led his skirmishing group out early on a June night of dense darkness that was in no way relieved by a clear sky that sparkled with stars. George Milnar and himself were the only two experienced men on the patrol, the five soldiers accompanying them being raw recruits. But they had been briefed long and in detail by the sergeant and himself. It was a vital mission so dangerous that Colonel Blueth had invited rather than ordered him to take it on. With the Union army short on intelligence regarding the deployment of Confederate troops, Anello was to move in close to the enemy lines at Little Round Top at Gettysburg to capture at least one Confederate officer and bring him back for questioning. Anello recognized that it was desperation and fear of further defeat that had his superiors promote this patrol. The chances of success were poor, and the possibility of survival for anyone on the patrol was even less hopeful. The objective, which lay some five thousand yards away, was a semi-derelict windmill. With them having been under heavy artillery fire, Colonel Blueth had concluded that the windmill was being used by forward observers, and the fire was so accurate that an officer was probably involved.

The importance of the mission was not lost on Anello. A victory in each and every battle was owed to the intelligence gained by the patrols preceding it. It was also a fact of life, or death, that patrol experience came at a high price. With a rare and paradoxical mixture of daring and caution, Sergeant Milnar was an ideal man to have along. Having reservations about the five young soldiers, Anello avoided prejudging them. Should they acquit themselves admirably, then he would see that they were rewarded within the military framework. If they failed him, then he would be equally determined to see that they received punishment in keeping with the effect such failure had on the patrol. All of them wore belts outside their tunics, with 'Arkansas toothpicks', long-bladed knives, thrust in them. Milnar and himself knew how to use theirs, and wouldn't hesitate to do so, but it took something that new recruits didn't usually have to knife a man to death.

Though conscious that they only had the hours of darkness in which to carry out the mission, Anello moved fairly slowly at first. This was to allow his detail to accustom themselves to the noises of the night. They had to learn how to pick out sounds that were man-made. It was likely that the Confederates, the enemy in the outposts they would approach, would have already taught themselves to do that.

On reaching the middle-ground he would speed up, but it would then be necessary to go slowly again. Great caution was needed because there was no such thing here as a stabilized front line. Opposing positions were so flexible that it was uncertain where friendly territory ended and the Confederate-held area began.

Avoiding all settlements, even the isolated farm house, Anello made good progress. Sooner than he had expected, he saw the black, disfigured silhouette of the crumbling windmill.

They all froze as a challenge was voiced, low and hoarsely, to their left. Able to sense the fear in the new recruits, Anello took comfort in the knowledge that George Milnar had prepared them for this. His guess was that the challenge was not directed at them, but a returning enemy patrol. All that was necessary for them to do was to wait out whatever it was.

Just minutes later they heard movement and guarded voices that proved his guess to have been correct. Moving off once more, Anello was aware of Milnar behind him signalling for the men to follow.

Close to the windmill, Anello dropped to the ground, with the sergeant coming down beside him. They were studying the apparently unoccupied building when one of the soldiers behind them accidentally caught the butt of his rifle against a tree. The resultant crack was so loud that it would carry far.

Within seconds Confederate rifles opened up.

Epitaph of Vengeance 117

Lead was whistling through the air, ripping through leaves, knocking branches from the trees around them. Then the firing suddenly ceased. Anello understood what was happening. Only suspecting that there were Union soldiers ahead of them in the darkness, the Confederates had fired in the hope that it would be returned, thereby confirming both the presence of the enemy and their position. Before leaving camp Anello had stressed that there would be no return fire unless he gave the order.

One member of his patrol was breathing fast and loudly, while another was mumbling prayers. Leaving Anello's side, Milnar crawled back to punch both men on the shoulder and gesture for them to stay silent. Back with Anello, he looked questioningly at him. The captain made hand movements that the sergeant immediately understood. They had to lie low until some diversion, such as another returning Confederate patrol, gave them the opportunity to move in on the windmill.

Time passed by with an agonizing slowness. Continually inspecting the sky, looking for any lightness to suggest a coming dawn, Anello realized that he was worrying unduly, for there were hours of the night yet to go. But nothing seemed to be happening, and he was aware that the nerves of the novice soldiers with him would become more strained with each passing minute.

Trying not to think of Loossantech, whose anger had moved her far from him, Anello wondered how Kansas was getting on at the Catholic settlement.

Despite the differences in the way they had lived their lives, he knew that she and Sister Joseph would get along well together. There was a lot of hard work to be done, and Kansas wouldn't shirk from doing it. Needing to assure Silver Moon that he hadn't abandoned her, that she would be fully avenged, he found that the dead Osage girl's face was indistinct in his mind. Each time he tried to conjure up Silver Moon, so did her beautiful sister appear. Wanting to see love in her dark eyes, Anello was devastated by the contempt for him that they still held.

A cautious nudge from Milnar's elbow instantly pushed the three women from his mind, bringing him alert. There was movement in the direction from which the shots had been fired at them. He could hear subdued voices, but was unable to decipher what was being said. At last they were being given a break. Another Confederate patrol had come back. Anello nodded to his sergeant. Milnar signalled to the men, and they were up and running toward the windmill.

Taking a wide arc, feet noiseless on soft grass, Anello had them skirt the building. A doorway with a door sagging crookedly on one hinge was at the front. They reached the rear of the windmill, all seven of them with their backs pressed tightly against the wall. Three figures came unexpectedly out of the night, heading for the windmill. Anello's sharp eyes used what light there was from the stars to identify the one in front as a lieutenant, followed by a sergeant and a private soldier. Turning his head to

Epitaph of Vengeance 119

Milnar, he saw his sergeant give a pleased little nod. By luck they had arrived at a time when the observers in the building were being relieved. There would be the same number of men, of the same rank, inside.

Things got even better then as Anello watched three men come out to the doorway to meet the newcomers.

'We heard shooting earlier,' the arriving officer said worriedly.

'That was just the shecoonery of them boys at the outposts,' the lieutenant coming out through the doorway explained. 'They're so danged scared that they shoot at a jack-rabbit's fart!'

Holding up a hand to stay Milnar and the others, Anello waited for the third man to step out of the mill. Only a few feet separated them from the six Confederates, but they needed them all to be outside. There were too many of them to take captive. Making a saluting motion, Anello held up two fingers before closing a finger and thumb together to form a circle. The sergeant got the message. They would take the two officers captive. Spreading three fingers on his left hand, Anello laid them against the upper part of his right sleeve. Then he took his hand away to hold up just one finger. George Milnar gave a nod of understanding. They would take just one sergeant prisoner. Making a slashing movement with the flat of his hand, Anello indicated that the remaining Confederates would be killed.

On Anello's silent signal they stepped out to take

the Confederates totally by surprise. Under the threat of Anello's rifle and that of a Union soldier, the two officers and one of the sergeants meekly went inside the windmill when a jerk of Anello's rifle ordered them to do so. Before going in the door himself, Anello turned his head to speak to his sergeant.

'Make it as quiet as you can, George,' he instructed softly. Inside he barked an order for the three Confederates to face the wall.

The young soldier with Anello was about eighteen years old, with the impoverished look of a kid from a New York slum. The knock-kneed way that he stood suggested rickets, and he was so frightened that he swallowed constantly and noisily. The sounds of scuffling from outside, and the sighing exhalation of breath by men dying, was affecting him badly.

'What's your name, soldier?' Anello enquired.

'B-b-b-b-enson, sir.'

'Well, Benson, hold that rifle steady and keep these three covered.'

Laying down his own rifle, Anello unwound twine that he had purposely tied around his waist. Cutting lengths off, he first approached the sergeant, a stocky man with wide shoulders and a brutishly prominent jaw. Placing the Confederate's hands behind his back, Anello lashed his wrists tightly before moving on to the first of the lieutenants.

'Don't tie them too tightly, son,' the lieutenant, an elderly man with a grey, drooping moustache advised when Anello pulled his thin wrists behind his back.

Epitaph of Vengeance

'You've got a long way to go back through our lines, and I want to be able to get myself free easily when you're dead.'

Not replying, Anello yanked the twine tightly so that it bit into the old man's skin, drawing a little blood. Ordinarily Anello was not a cruel man, but there was a lot of truth in what the Confederate had said. Luck had been with them on the way out, but there was no guarantee it would hold on the way back.

Having been looking sideways at Anello, the other lieutenant jerked his head back to face the wall as he came up, the final length of twine at the ready. As Anello wrapped the rope round his wrists, the lieutenant chuckled so deeply that his body shook.

'Well don't that cap the climax! Don't that beat all!' the Confederate wagged his head from side to side as he exclaimed, 'You didn't rightly seem like no cattleman to me, but danged if I placed you as a Yankee captain!'

Stopping tying the wrists, Anello reached out a hand to the Confederate officer's shoulder to pull him partly round. He gasped in surprise, 'Jonathan Forrest!'

'We drank together, August,' the Confederate said with a friendly smile, his head half turned from the wall. 'That sure has to mean something.'

'Not as much as war does,' Anello told him dully, turning his face back to the wall.

'I guess not,' Forrest said resignedly as Anello tied his wrists, tightly.

When they went outside with the bound prisoners, Milnar had laid the bodies of the other Confederates tidily against the wall of the building. But there was the stench of human blood on the air, and one of the Union soldiers was clinging to a tree for support as he bent over, vomiting. Some of the others were watching their retching comrade sympathetically. It was a situation in which cowardice could thrive. They were behind enemy lines, and it would take real soldiers to get safely back. Anello snapped an order at Milnar.

'Beat that Nancy-boy into shape, Sergeant, now!'

'Sir,' Milnar acknowledged the order, striding over to the soldier who was still sick.

'You can shout at them, beat them, whip them, Captain, but you can't place courage where it doesn't belong,' the elderly Confederate officer said quietly. 'My left ear has done more soldiering than that poor boy will ever do.'

'What are you, some kind of Philadelphia lawyer?' Anello asked, relieved as he saw that Milnar had the soldier moving.

'Indeed not, sir,' the lieutenant answered, long grey hair falling almost to his shoulders because his hat had somehow been knocked sideways. 'I am simply an observer of the human race, and I must say that we really are a sorry lot.'

'We're going back now, so all you need to do is to keep your mouth shut, old man,' Anello said, not unkindly, finding himself putting the Confederate's hat straight for him, but not knowing why he did it.

Epitaph of Vengeance

Having been a serving soldier since a boy, Anello had never been able to completely come to terms with killing. He found that the elderly officer's comment on the human race had profoundly depressed him.

'It would be foolish for any of us to make a noise, Captain, for a bullet cannot tell friend from foe in the dark,' the elderly lieutenant pointed out as Anello lined them up to move off.

He took the point once more, with Sergeant Milnar behind him, then four of his soldiers. The three prisoners followed, with Benson, ordered to watch them carefully, bringing up the rear.

Deciding to take them back on a different route to the one he had used coming out, a precaution should their presence have been detected and an ambush laid for their return, Anello was making good time until reaching a large, wide open field. With them crouching beside bushes surrounding the field, he explained what he wanted. There was no time to crawl, so the field had to be crossed at a run. Anello would go first with the others covering him. When he reached the far side he would watch over Milnar as he ran. The others would come next, covered by Anello and Milnar, with Benson bringing up the rear behind the prisoners.

Crawling to where that soldier crouched, Anello whispered close to his ear, 'Watch them, Benson. This will be their best chance of escape.'

'Sir,' Benson, looking far from confident, acknowledged the order.

Back at the head of the line, Anello used a short movement of an arm to let Milnar know he was going. Aware that he was taking the main risk, for if the Confederates were lying in wait they would fire on the first man, he started to run.

Three-quarters of the way across the field he dropped flat as the leaves of bushes up ahead rattled. Lying with his rifle to his shoulder, Anello watched where the noise had come from, expecting a shot, or most probably a fusillade, at any second. He hoped that Milnar's sharp eyes could see enough in the dark so that he didn't begin the run himself.

Finger tightening on the trigger as another slight sound came from the bushes, Anello felt foolish as he heard a flapping of wings and an owl hooted. Cursing himself for behaving like a recruit yet to go through his baptism of fire, he got up and made it to the bushes without further incident.

Sergeant Milnar made it safely, and then the others were on the run. Head close to the ground so as to be able to see better in the night, Anello watched them come. He held his breath as he saw the Confederate sergeant break out of the line to run off at an angle. About to send Milnar after him, he was astounded to see Benson go into action. With a surprising alacrity, the scrawny soldier thrust his rifle between the legs of the absconding prisoner, sending him crashing to the ground. Reaching down to catch the sergeant by the collar, Benson dragged him to his feet and slung him back into line.

'Well done, son,' Anello praised the boy when all

Epitaph of Vengeance

of them, including the prisoners, were safely across the field.

They were moving through scrub then, not far from their own lines. Falling out, signalling for Milnar to take the lead, Anello dropped back to take Forrest out of the line, gesturing for Benson to close up and keep moving.

The Confederate lieutenant stood waiting silently in the darkness as Anello took his knife from his belt. Stepping close, he slashed the rope that bound Forrest's hands behind his back. Rubbing his wrists to assist the blood to circulate after the restriction of the twine, the Confederate gave Anello a grin that showed through the night.

Speaking softly, Anello said, 'I never forget a friend or an enemy.'

'Which of those two things do you see me as, August?' Forrest whispered his question.

'Let's just say that I hope to be able to buy you a drink when this is all over, Jonathan.'

'Thanks, and good luck,' the Confederate said, shaking Anello by the hand. '*Hasta la vista*, as our Mexican friends say.'

'*Haste la vista, amigo*,' Anello, made a little sad by the parting, replied as the Confederate moved off into the darkness.

Going back to take the point, Anello led until they reached a point where Milnar needed to go on ahead to warn their own outposts that they were coming back in. Receiving his instructions from Anello, the sergeant spoke quietly and confidentially to him.

'I notice that one of the captives has escaped, sir.'

Milnar was too astute not to know that Anello had released the Confederate officer, and would have accepted that the captain had a good reason for doing so. The sergeant just wanted it to be known that he was conversant with what was going on around him.

'Check again, George,' Anello advised. 'I could never fault you as a soldier, but your counting can't be relied on.'

An agitated Benson came hesitantly up to them. Having seen Anello take one of his prisoners away and not bring him back, the young soldier was in a dilemma. Unsure how to broach the subject, he made everything worse for himself by stammering badly when he reported that he could not find one of the Confederate officer prisoners.

'You've proved tonight that you have the makings of a good soldier, Benson,' Sergeant Milnar drily remarked, 'but you sure are poor shakes at counting!'

As his sergeant went off toward their own lines, leaving behind a now totally bewildered Benson, Anello permitted himself a smile. The night had gone real well, all in all, and Jonathan Forrest's handshake had done much to alleviate the gloom that had come with the elderly Confederate's critical observation on people in general.

Eight

The Confederate artillery barrage had gone on relentlessly for thirty-six hours. With it beginning just after they had been reinforced by seven companies of infantry under a Major McKenzie, Union casualties had at first been heavy. But they had dug in and now little damage was being done except for the effect the constant shelling was having on the nerves of the men. The success of Anello's prisoner-taking patrol meant that the barrage had been expected. The elderly officer had given his name as Zachary Belmont, and his rank as that of lieutenant, but would say no more. It was the captured sergeant who volunteered to give information on the strength and deployment of his own army. His initial motive was to save his life, which he had believed was under threat. But then he had continued to talk after being promised that it would guarantee favourable treatment as a prisoner-of-war.

Through him they knew the exact positions of the Confederate forces, but this was of no use to them while the artillery had them pinned down. Most dangerous of all the Confederate ammunition were the tin canisters filled with iron balls. Fired from cannon, the massive scatter-gun-like effect of these canisters was devastating.

It was through the canister hazard, as well as ordinary artillery shells, that Captain Anello made his way to Colonel Blueth after having been summoned by a runner.

'I'm afraid you've drawn the short end of the horn once more, August,' Blueth spoke through a background of shattering noise, raising his voice when necessary so as to be heard. 'They have the upper hand so long as they have us totally disabled by their artillery. It's not going to be easy, but we have to break out. We must take the fight to them, Captain.'

You mean *I* have to take the fight to them, Anello said inside his head. Yet he instantly regretted such bitter thinking. Colonel Blueth's position of command meant he needed to do the planning at that time while he had someone else do the fighting. It wasn't a matter of choice, for Blueth was a brave man. When the real battle began the Colonel would be out there ahead of his men.

'What are my orders, sir?' Anello stood to attention as he asked.

'They are orders that I would avoid giving if it were at all possible, August,' Blueth said, his face registering the sincere regret that he was feeling. 'I have already asked more of you than can be expected from any one officer. We have to get our artillery up to Cemetery Ridge and commence return fire.'

Something deep inside Anello momentarily objected. It was a brief but demoralizing experience for a man who had no idea that such naked fear lurked within him. But then it was gone and he was a competent officer once more.

He said, 'If it can be done, sir, then I'll do it.'

'That is why I selected you, August. May God go with you,' the Colonel said, his face sombre as he returned Anello's smart salute.

Running off, in a straight line because there was no way to judge where the next shell might land, Anello made it to where Sergeant Milnar crouched in a dug-out. Jumping in beside the sergeant, Anello pressed his back against the wall of the trench to wait while a shell whistled past, low and close to them.

'I got a feeling that I ain't going to like what you're about to tell me, sir,' Milnar muttered in a morose but philosophical manner.

'I'm here to offer you a choice, George,' Anello said with a grim smile. 'You can either stay here and maybe get your butt blown off, or....'

'Or follow you and definitely get it blown off,' the sergeant, already climbing up out of the dug-out, anticipated the second choice the captain was offering.

Together they dodged among falling shells to rally men who wanted only to hide away in safety, as if the war was a bad dream that would end without any action by them. Both the captain and the sergeant were aware that it was necessary to make the soldiers more afraid of them than they were the shelling. It was an easier task once they had the bravest men showing the others the way. Frightened horses added their squealing and snorting to the noise of the artillery. Made dangerous by panic, the horses fought all the way as they were harnessed to gun carriages. Benson was there, making a commendable effort. Not far from Anello, he gave the captain a tentative smile. Anello smiled back. For all his poor physique and impoverished look, the New York boy was proving himself to be a fine soldier.

They'd had the usual Napoleon twelve-pound, smoothbore cannon replaced by the three-inch U.S. rifle. This was a wrought-iron artillery gun that had a greater range and was far more accurate than the Napoleon. Aware that the new gun had teething problems that often had it malfunction at vital moments, Anello was content that they had enough of the guns to make up for that defect.

A caisson was hitched up and the first gun carriage was ready to lead the way. Mindless of the gunfire now that they were busy, the soldiers moved the other carriages into line. A trooper on a saddled horse would ride beside the two battery horses hitched to each gun carriage, leading them. They took up positions as, side by side, Milnar and Anello mounted up, the latter giving the order to move out.

The carriage wheels had rolled only a few feet when a shell exploded as it hit the off-wheel horse of the first gun carriage. The horse was torn to bits. Bloody pieces of it flew everywhere, some splattering

Epitaph of Vengeance 131

over horrified soldiers. The saddle horse was mangled by the bursting shell, too, and the man on its back tumbled to the ground, dead.

The nerve of one soldier on a saddle horse broke completely. Wheeling his horse around, he galloped off. Obeying army rules where a deserter is concerned, Sergeant Milnar drew his rifle ready to shoot the man out of the saddle

Reaching out a hand to stay his sergeant, Anello said, 'Let him go, George. We might well all be doing the same as he is before this hour is over.'

The shelling seemed to have increased, giving a greater urgency to the operation. With the shattered horse cut free of the carriage and another animal harnessed up, none of the soldiers, understandably, seemed willing to take the lead. Anello was about to issue further orders when Benson saved him from doing so. Riding up, the New York soldier leaned over in the saddle to take charge of the fresh horses that had been hitched to the first gun carriage. With shells bursting all around him, Benson led the carriage on, his cool action encouraging the other soldiers to follow.

Relieved to see the line of artillery rolling, and proud of the young soldier, Anello moved on ahead, George Milnar at his side. They were close to the top of the hill, and although the Confederate fire had not lessened in the least, they had been untouched since the first tragedy.

But then the third carriage in the line received a direct hit. The horses had been playing up, and the soldier leading them had dismounted to control them by walking by the side of the carriage. One horse was blown to smithereens, and the white horse at its side instantly became a bay as it was painted red by the blood of its companion. The right foot of the walking soldier had been blown off. He stood stock still, looking down in shock at where the foot used to be. Realization and pain hit the man at the same time, and he went round in crazy circles, awkwardly stumbling this way and that on a white bone of a stump.

'Keep them coming!' Anello shouted, waving his men on, aware that under the merciless fire their next move could be an involuntary retreat.

Milnar was riding in and out of the carriages, yelling, 'Keep up, you men.'

They were at the top of the hill now, and were receiving more hits. Confusion was growing all around him when Anello dismounted to organize the guns into firing positions. It was a flat piece of heavily wooded ground. Shells ripping away the tops of trees made an awesome sound that vastly amplified the artillery noise. He saw the courageous Benson leading the first carriage into what would be the best firing position. Anello cried out, his yell of despair snatched away in the general noise, as he saw Benson, who had been about to dismount, reel in the saddle as he and his horse were hit. Benson's right arm, torn away from his thin body, flew up to collide against a tree before falling back to the ground. The New York boy and his horse went down, the animal staying there, but the soldier somehow got to his feet. He took a few steps toward Anello, who had the ridiculous impression that Benson's last act was to try to salute him by using the arm that he no longer had. But the boy, dead on his feet, just crumpled into a messy heap on the ground.

Milnar had taken over Benson's gun carriage, cutting a badly injured horse free. Groaning piteously, blood pouring from where its lower jaw had been shot away, the horse staggered up to Anello. On what was left of the horse's face was the beseeching look of a child wanting to be cuddled. It was begging for help that Anello couldn't give. Despising the situation, hating himself, Anello drew his Colt, put the muzzle between the eyes of the stricken animal, and pulled the trigger.

He ran to Milnar's side. The sergeant's face and uniform were covered with blood, but the active way he moved told Anello that it was the blood of other men and horses, not Milnar's own.

Needing to inspire the men, they got the gun firing. There were more casualties behind them, men who were wounded crying out, men who were dying doing so quietly in some cases, but in others their last agonies had them scream out horrendously.

Yet soon every gun capable of firing was spitting ball and flame. Other soldiers had come up behind on foot to unhitch the caissons and bring ammunition round to within easy reach of the gunners. Within a short time the Union barrage was superior to that of the Confederates, and the latter was abating.

Everything was going well. At last the enemy was under heavy fire, getting a taste of their own medicine. Anello was sending a runner back to have Colonel Blueth move to go over Cemetery Ridge and down the slopes to engage the Confederates, when Milnar ran toward him with the bad news. The enemy was moving in behind, outflanking them, cutting them off from Blueth and the main force.

Anello's first reaction was to consider turning half his number of guns to fire back down the hill behind them. He had to cancel this plan when the rattle of small-arms fire came up to him. Colonel Blueth had engaged the Confederates, and for Anello to bring his artillery into play would be to kill friend as well as foe.

Dashing about, Anello ordered his gun crews to continue firing. Then he had every saddle horse rounded up, with a soldier allocated to each one. Shouting above the deafening roar of his own guns, he told the mounted men what was happening behind them, and explained that he was leading them on an attack that would force the enemy to face two fronts.

Rising up in his stirrups he yelled, 'Remember this is the Sixth Kansas Cavalry! Men, follow me!'

At a breakneck speed, his sword in his hand and his sergeant beside him, Anello led his squad down the hill. The attack took the Confederates completely by surprise. Having his men hold their fire until they had ridden in close, he gave the order to open up and the Confederates were mown down

Epitaph of Vengeance 135

in what was a massacre on a modest but devastating scale.

Slashing and thrusting with his sword, Anello rode straight in to take on the enemy at close-quarters. He saw Milnar using his revolver and kicks from a foot he had freed from the stirrup to down the enemy. His men were making dual use of their standard issue Colt revolvers by either firing them or clubbing the Confederates in hand to hand fighting. It saddened Anello to watch four of his soldiers go down in as many seconds, but the Confederates were giving way.

'Lieutenant Mallory! Lieutenant Mallory, sir!'

From close by, Anello heard this urgent shout rise above the many-sounded, discordant roar of battle. It was the officer's name that instantly captured his attention. Easily beating off a clumsy, one-man attack being made on him, he looked to see a young Confederate soldier edging his mount through the fighting to where one of his officers stood beside a fallen horse, exposed to danger.

It was the soldier's intention to have the Confederate officer, a young, handsome man, get up on the horse behind him so that they could ride double out of a battle that was already lost.

Forcing his horse in close while the Confederate officer was still on foot, Anello thrust his sword with such force into the chest of the soldier on the horse that he was impaled. It took all of Anello's strength to pull the weapon free. By that time Lieutenant Mallory was fleeing through the wheeling, rearing horses, but he tripped over some dead bodies. As the Confederate officer recovered his balance, Anello swept in on his horse, his sword, razor-sharp, swinging in an arc to slice through the back of Mallory's neck. As he straightened up in the saddle to ride on, Anello saw Loossantech's beautiful face in his head. The Osage girl gave him a smile of gratitude.

In the acrid stench of cordite the ferocity of the fighting lessened. With the enemy withdrawing fast, Anello saw more blue coats among the grey, which told him that the Union's main force was breaking through. Coming through a heavy curtain of gunsmoke, face blackened by gunpowder, Colonel Blueth rode up to Anello.

'Well done, Captain Anello!' the colonel shouted, wearing the first smile that Anello had ever seen on his face. 'It's a complete rout. Our grandchildren will never believe us when we tell them of today!'

Without even attempting a rearguard action, the remnants of the Confederate force were fleeing in the direction from which they had come. From high up on the ridge came the steady, heavy pounding of Union guns. Blueth, euphoria still brightening his eyes, but his speech and manner having regained his customary reserve, moved his horse closer to Anello.

'The day is not yet done, Captain,' the Colonel said. 'We are going up and over Cemetery Ridge.' Pausing, he reached into his coat to bring out a small flask, which he held out to Anello. 'Whiskey, Captain. Take it with you, August, and drink a toast to our victory when it is achieved.'

Epitaph of Vengeance 137

Officers, commissioned and non-commissioned, were yelling orders then to restore formation, order and discipline now that the fighting was over. Anello, Milnar and the troopers they had brought down from the ridge stayed mounted to fall in behind Colonel Blueth. Major McKenzie and his foot-soldiers, who would play an important follow-up role in the fight to come, brought up the rear. The Union army of cavalry and foot started up the hill at a dignified pace that had the look of a military ritual performed at a tattoo rather than an attacking force. The contradiction in the appearance of the troop and what it was heading toward was disturbing for Anello.

The relaxed atmosphere was dissolved by tension as they went over the ridge. With Colonel Blueth, in his element, at their head, their own shells hissing through the air over their heads, and a moderate amount of fire still coming from Confederate guns, they awaited the order.

It came with Blueth rising up in his stirrups and turning to face them. Drawing his sword, the colonel held it high as he screamed out the order: 'Charge!'

Pouring withering fire ahead of them, they galloped down the slope. But the Confederates had fooled them by having closed down more than half of their cannon. Once the Union charge had gained enough momentum so that it couldn't be stopped, the enemy artillery went fully into action. On Anello's right he saw a shell scythe through first Union cavalry and then the infantry, knocking rows of men down as if in some amusing game. Their ranks were being ripped apart.

To his left a cannon ball passed through Colonel Blueth's right thigh, on through the body of his horse and then his other thigh. Made legless instantly, the colonel toppled from his horse. Reining his horse to the left, Anello prevented the horses coming behind from trampling on Blueth. But when he reached where the colonel lay he could do nothing but sit in the saddle and stare at the ghastly sight of a trunk, two arms and a head from which the eyes protruded horribly. Blueth was bleeding so copiously that he would die within minutes, if he were not already dead.

Knowing that there was nothing he could do for his commanding officer, apart from gaining victory, Anello sent his horse off in a gallop down the slope.

Once the Union troops had passed through the artillery, the Confederates realized that their daring attack was doomed; over. Sword drawn for the second time within an hour or two, Anello rode into combat. There was gunfire, yelling, shouting, screaming and cursing as the battle continued. But then a change could be sensed as the Confederates fell back. Then they were running, followed by Union troops who hooted and hollered in triumph.

But it was a pointless pursuit and Anello reined up to look around for the bugler to sound recall. That soldier was either dead or part of the victorious Union group chasing the Confederates.

Finding himself alone in a field of carnage, Anello

Epitaph of Vengeance 139

dismounted to stroll unhappily through the mangled, cut or shot bodies that, some in blue, others in grey, lay around with their arms, legs and heads in peculiar positions. Young eyes that had sought a drink or looked for a woman, now stared at death. The lucky ones looked up at the sky, while the less fortunate gazed sightlessly at the corpse lying beside them.

His thoughts were for George Milnar. Praying that the sergeant had survived, Anello checked the blue-coated bodies, fearing that the next one he looked at would be that of his friend. Milnar wasn't there, but there was something familiar about the body of a Confederate that was lying face down.

Hunkering to reach out and catch hold of a shoulder to tilt the body, Anello went icy cold as he found himself looking into the dead eyes of Lieutenant Jonathan Forrest.

Standing upright, ashamed to find himself near to tears, Anello took from his pocket the flask given to him by Colonel Blueth. Uncorking the flask, he held it up in front of him, saying, 'To victory, and to you, Colonel Blueth!'

Drinking deep, Anello replaced the cork in the flask and went down on one knee to roll Forrest onto his back. Crossing the Confederate's hands over his chest, Anello put the flask into one of them, curling the stiffening fingers so that they held it.

'That's the drink I owe you, Jonathan,' Anello said quietly, tears blurring his eyes so that even if he had turned round he wouldn't have clearly seen the terribly wounded Confederate soldier who had sat up and was pointing a rifle at him.

The Confederate fired the last shot of the battle, and August Anello slumped forward to lie at the side of Jonathan Forrest.

Nine

Once welcome because it had relieved his pain and eased his total weariness, the bed had become a prison for August Anello as he recovered from his injury. He had learned that Sergeant George Milnar had found him, mistakenly believing that he belonged with all the other dead. But a weak pulse had been beating in the captain's neck, and Milnar had called for help. The Confederate bullet had lodged in Anello's chest, so close to the heart that surgery came closer to killing him than the enemy had.

This morning he had been allowed out of bed for the first time. Joining the walking wounded, his help was enlisted for a number of chores because the field hospital had been plunged into turmoil by notice that a general was about to pay a visit. Fearing an in-depth inspection, the hospital staff was in a state of abject panic.

An hour later, Anello was standing beside his bed as Major-General George G. Meade and his entourage entered. Stern of face, the general paused at each bed to have a gruff word with the wounded man who either lay in or stood beside it. Some were in too bad a way to know that the general was there, and Meade stood mutely looking down at them for a minute or so. He appeared to be considerably moved by the sight of these badly injured patients. On reaching Anello, Meade stood unspeaking, studying him so intently that it seemed to Anello that the general was attempting to read his thoughts. He became uncomfortable, as did the officers accompanying Meade, but eventually the general did speak.

'Colonel Anello, am I right?' General Meade said.

'Captain Anello, sir,' Anello corrected him.

'The day that I need a captain to put me right on anything, Anello,' the general said brusquely, although it seemed there was a twinkle somewhere deep in his eyes, 'is the day I will hang up my uniform.'

Patients and staff were listening, enthralled by the situation. Meade appeared to be in no hurry to move on from Anello's bed, and as the general was well known for his belligerence, many of the spectators anticipated fireworks, with Anello for some reason the victim of Meade's ready anger.

'I don't understand, sir,' Anello said, not knowing what to expect next.

The hard lines of General Meade's face softened slightly. 'I know that you don't understand, son. It wasn't finalized till late yesterday, but I'm here to inform you of your promotion to lieutenant-colonel.'

Anello was taken aback. This was totally unexpected. His elation was tamped down by the realization that he had been promoted to take the place of Colonel Blueth.

'I take it that the effects of your injury prevent you from fully appreciating this,' a disappointed general commented.

'I do appreciate the promotion, sir, and it makes me proud,' Anello replied, 'but I'd prefer Colonel Blueth to have lived.'

Moving closer, a trace of anger in his voice, Meade said, 'Now, you listen to me, Colonel. Had Colonel Blueth not died in the field, you would have been promoted beside him. You more than earned your promotion at Cemetery Ridge, Anello.'

This made Anello feel better, and he was able to return Meade's smile when the general shook him by the hand.

'You are a fine soldier, Colonel, but you are lacking something,' Meade paused as he started to move away.

'What is that, sir?' Anello enquired.

Giving him a friendly punch on the shoulder, Meade told him. 'You need the stabilizing influence of a wife, Colonel. It isn't right for an officer of your age not to be wed. Find yourself a good woman, son.'

When the general had gone, Anello pondered on his parting words, though suspecting that he might have spoken in jest. Whatever, the message was plain. Meade envisaged that, as a married man, August Anello would reach the top in the army. The problem was that the general would be far from impressed if Anello were to present a whore or an Osage squaw as his future wife, and Sister Joseph, who would be seen as the ideal army officer's wife, had a vocation that she would ever refuse to abandon.

This inconclusive reasoning was complicated further when he received another visitor later in the day. This time it was a civilian, a tall, strange-looking figure in a long, black cloak. Anello was mystified on recognizing the colporteur who had handed him pamphlets just prior to the battle.

'I am pleased to find you so well, brother,' the tall man said in a sepulchre voice when reaching Anello's bed. With a long, bony face, the religious man was so ill at ease in the situation that he looked ready to flee.

'Who are you?' a puzzled Anello asked.

'They call me Peter,' the man replied in a way that inferred he didn't know he had a name until 'they' gave him one. He self-consciously passed a small package to Anello, saying, 'It is well known that the food here is austere. Here is a small treat for you.'

Unwrapping the paper package, Anello discovered that it contained six molasses cookies. He said, 'This is very kind of you, but you didn't come here just to bring me food, did you?'

Shaking his permanently sad head, Peter admit-

Epitaph of Vengeance

ted, 'No, the Osage girl, Loossantech, asked me to deliver a message. I am to tell you that the man you seek, the last man, is living with his wife close to the mission of Sister Joseph.'

Yet again Anello was astounded by the way the Osage collected and passed on information. It seemed impossible, but Loossantech knew that he had killed Mallory on the battlefield. Now she was applying pressure to have him go after the last man of the group responsible for the death of her sister. Once out of hospital, with at least a short period of sick-leave due to him, he would seek out Siegle. But he would do so for Silver Moon, not for Loossantech. Not only that, but Anello would reluctantly carry out the final act of vengeance, for of late he'd had enough of killing.

'How much do you know of this, Peter?' he enquired.

'I have been told nothing,' Peter replied, 'but I am very aware that you are approaching an important point in your life.'

'How would you know that?'

Looking steadily at Anello, the tall, thin man replied softly, 'I know many things. You will very soon have to make a decision. Make the wrong one and you are doomed.'

'So,' Anello said, shaken by what the odd man had said, 'tell me what is the right thing for me to do?'

'That I cannot do, brother,' Peter looked sympathetically at him.

'You could at least advise,' Anello complained.

'Everything seems to be jumbled up inside my head.'

Tapping his own forehead with a finger, Peter told him, 'You will not find the answer up here.' He then placed his hand flat on his chest. 'It is in your heart that you will find what you seek.'

Anello opened his mouth to make an enquiry, but his visitor was leaving him.

'I will be praying for you, brother,' Peter said, drifting away as creepily as a ghost.

Left alone, Anello sat morosely, pulled mentally this way and that by four women, one of them dead, three alive. It occurred to him that the war still raged on, and that he would soon be back in the thick of it. A Confederate bullet in his brain would solve everything for him. But that would be no real answer.

With something in addition to the magic Silver Moon had held for him, Loossantech offered everything he could want in a woman. Some part of his own self needed to be complemented by the untameable nature of a savage. Her being an Osage was not too much of an obstacle. There was no way to disguise that she was an Indian, but her beauty and grace would have her scrape through as the wife of a colonel. General Meade had nothing to do with what he was thinking. Anello had long been aware that he needed a partner in life, and would have married Silver Moon by now had it not been for her tragic death.

His mood blackened until all gloom was lifted from him by the sight of George Milnar walking in, wearing the uniform and insignia of a lieutenant.

Epitaph of Vengeance

'George, you've made it! Well done!' he joyfully greeted his friend. 'Congratulations.'

'And to you, Colonel, sir,' Milnar said. 'I know that I owe everything to you.'

'Nonsense!' Anello scoffed at the suggestion. 'Sit down, George, and brief me on what is going on out there in the world.'

Sitting stiffly, not feeling at home in either his new uniform or the surroundings, Milnar brought Anello up to date on the military situation. By all accounts Confederates were on the run. After the damage inflicted on him at Gettysburg, General Lee had rapidly fallen back to Virginia, while at the same time Ulysses S. Grant had taken the Confederate stronghold of Vicksburg on the Mississippi for the Union.

'There's preparation now for a winter campaign on two fronts, sir,' Lieutenant Milnar concluded. 'The Union Army of the Tennessee is heading under Sherman for Atlanta and beyond, while we'll be moving into northern Virginia with General Grant. I take it you'll be fit soon, sir?'

'I'll be out of here in a day or so, George,' Anello assured his friend. While the two of them had been discussing the coming offensive, the bloody, body-smashing, ear-shattering factors of war were pleasantly remote. But Anello was well aware of how quickly they would become a stark reality. He added, 'I will be away for a short time, George. I still have some personal business to take care of.'

'Take care, sir,' Milnar cautioned. 'A one-man

vendetta can be just as dangerous as a full-scale battle.'

'And equally distressing,' Anello gave a nod of agreement as he spoke from the heart.

Ten

Dismounting, Anello walked toward the mission. With exertion bringing pain to his not fully healed chest, he had ridden through a purple twilight that had a profound effect on him. On a similar night, shortly before her passing, Silver Moon had sung a song as they had sat together beside a placid lake. Able only to understand a few of the Osage words, it had sounded to him like a dirge. When he had gently questioned her, she had refused to say what message the song held. This had him wonder if the Indian girl he loved had foreseen her own death, and it worried him that his recalling the song now might be an omen for the immediate future. But he put his dark mood down to loneliness when Sister Joseph opened the door as he approached. The apprehension on her face changed to a radiant smile as she recognized him.

'Where are the other two?' Sister Joseph enquired.

Taking a glance behind him, Anello said, 'I don't understand, Sister Joseph.'

'Forgive me, August, I am being sacrilegious,' the nun said with a sweet, tinkling laugh. 'You see, we have a birth due at any moment.' She put a small hand on his arm. 'We'll have to make do with one wise man. You are most welcome, August.'

Moved by sudden impulse, Anello dropped to one knee, asking, 'Bless me, Sister.'

Making the sign of the cross over his bowed head, Sister Joseph studied his face as he stood. 'You are a troubled man, August.'

'It will pass,' he assured her as they walked slowly together toward the door.

'We have a farmer's wife from the valley in our little schoolroom, and our humble building is about to be glorified by the birth of a child, August,' Sister Joseph said happily, but her face went serious as she prevented him from going in the door. 'The father of the child is, I believe, a man that you seek.'

'His name, Sister Joseph?' Anello tersely asked.

'He is called Antony Siegle, August. His wife is Maria,' Sister Joseph said. 'He will be riding in to see his wife within the hour. What will you do, August?'

'What would you have me do, Sister Joseph?' he asked glumly. 'What is the right thing to do?'

'You will no doubt see it differently to me.'

'Which one of us has it right, Sister?' Anello asked almost pleadingly.

'Maybe neither of us,' the nun replied with a wistful smile. 'You must do as you see fit, August. Now, come inside, there is someone who will be very pleased to see you.'

Epitaph of Vengeance

'Kansas!' he said, suddenly warmed by the thought of meeting the plucky Kansas Withers again.

Sister Joseph gave a happy little nod. 'Kansas is a good woman, a hard worker, August. It has been a joy for us all to have her here.'

They were inside then, and he was disappointed to find the place empty, but the nun at his side pointed to the door at the end of the room, saying, 'Kansas is helping with the birth. I will tell her you are here, August.'

Within minutes Kansas had come through the door and was running toward him, stopping abruptly a few feet from him as if colliding with an invisible barrier. Hair awry, she brushed it back from her forehead with one hand, suddenly becoming diffident in his presence.

'It is good to see you again, August,' she said, eyes downcast.

'And you, Kansas,' he said, remembering what they had shared together, saddened by the knowledge that it would never happen again, that they must both go their separate ways in life. Clasping her shoulders, he held her at arm's length. 'I will be leaving here for good in the morning, Kansas. In what way can I help you before I go?'

Whatever was to happen with Siegle, and in spite of Sister Joseph and the circumstances, he couldn't see any way that he could not completely avenge Silver Moon. His only course was to make the last man pay, then return to Loossantech. If the Indian girl would have him, then he would make her his wife either before or after riding out with General Grant.

'I am not your responsibility, August,' Kansas told him bravely, though he could see tears glistening in her eyes.

'Each of us has a responsibility to the other,' Anello said.

'You have learned well during the short visits you have paid us, August,' Sister Joseph, who he hadn't heard approach, said with a touch of levity. 'I have your supper ready. Kansas, the sisters need you. The birth is very close.'

Releasing Kansas, Anello walked, heavy-footed, to the table on which Sister Joseph had placed a plate of food. She left him to eat alone. As he did so he heard a woman groaning. There was a small scream of half pain, half joy, then the lusty crying of a newborn baby. His meal finished, Anello stood and walked out into the night to do some thinking.

Leaning over the rail of a fence the nuns had constructed to contain a milch cow, he tried to relax. There was a quarter-moon and millions of twinkling stars in a peaceful sky. Enjoying the serenity of the night, he heard a rider approach, dismount, and go running into the building.

Anello didn't look behind him as the door closed and he heard limping footsteps coming his way. His name was spoken as a question. 'Anello?'

Turning his head, Anello saw a stocky young man, a man born to plough the land, looking fearfully at him. He said, 'I'm Anello.'

'I'm Antony Siegle, and I know why you're here,' Siegle's voice was sorrowful.

'To kill you,' Anello confirmed in a flat voice.

'I'm ready to die for what happened, but I want to say I had nothing to do with it. I tried to stop the others. I'm not asking you to believe me. Neither am I begging for my life. All I want is to set the record straight. When you've afterwards, I'd be mighty obliged if you had the sisters tell Maria what I just said to you, and have her tell my boy the same thing when he's old enough to understand.'

Turning to lean his back against the rail, Anello said, 'Step away, Siegle, and I'll let you slap leather first.'

Shaking his close-cropped head, Siegle protested, 'I ain't going for my gun. This ain't no gunfight, mister, it's an execution, and you're the executioner.'

'I don't know why, Siegle,' Anello murmured, something about the young fellow impressing him, 'but I do believe that you're saying the truth. Go back in there to that son of yours. I will never bother. . . .'

There was a blur of action then. Catching the sound of metal scraping against the bark of a tree, Anello gave Siegle a push that sent him sprawling as there came the crack of a rifle and a bullet spat through the air where he had been standing. Spinning on his heel, Anello drew and fired at a slender oak some yards off. A figure leaned slowly out from behind the trunk, then flopped to the ground.

Hurrying over, gun still in his hand, a mortified

Anello half collapsed, needing to lean against the tree, as he found himself looking down at the body of Loossantech, a dark stain on her skin shirt spreading right across her chest. He cursed his own reflexes for having him react so fast. The Osage girl had obviously tracked down Siegle. When she'd heard Anello reprieve the man, she had decided to deal with Siegle herself. It grieved Anello that he had killed her.

Kansas was coming slowly toward him. Not having heard the door open, Anello assumed she had been outside throughout the incident. An uncertain Siegle stayed back in the shadows.

Looking down at the dead Loossantech, Kansas, tears streaming down her face, held out a rifle to Anello, saying, so softly that he barely caught her words, 'I couldn't let you kill her.'

Allowing his memory to piece the incident together correctly in his mind, Anello remembered hearing a third shot close to his own. Looking at the tree, he saw where his bullet had run a furrow through the bark. For the first time ever he had been off target. It was something he would eternally be grateful for.

He said sombrely, 'I'll have to take you in, Kansas.'

'I know,' she replied submissively, then walked back to the building with her head bowed.

Sister Joseph and the other nuns left him alone as he knelt for a long time beside Loossantech. When he walked to find a shovel, Siegle offered to help dig the grave. Thanking him, Anello refused the offer.

Epitaph of Vengeance 155

Going to a grassy slope that was prettily fringed by palmetto trees, he worked fast.

When her place of rest was ready, and he carried Loossantech to it, the nuns drifted up through the night to stand by the graveside. Sister Joseph led the prayers. Anello saw a sorrowing Kansas joining in from where she stood at the back of the group. They sang a short, poignant hymn, then left him to finish his task.

Sister Joseph met him when he went into the building, passing him a glass filled with an amber liquid. He took a sip to discover that it was whiskey.

'For medicinal purposes,' she told him with a sad smile, then she left him alone, saying, 'Good night, and may God bless you, August Anello.'

Sitting at a table, Anello slowly drank the whiskey. Siegle was somewhere in the building with his wife and new-born child, safe from Anello who knew in his heart that Silver Moon would want there to be no more killing. In his grief his half-numbed mind found it difficult to comprehend that he hadn't killed Loossantech. That fact slowly seeped in, allowing him to sleep, head in hands that rested on the table, less than an hour before dawn.

Sister Joseph wakened him in the morning. He drank strong black coffee but turned down the nun's offer of a cooked breakfast. Walking to the door with him when he was ready to leave, she said tearfully, 'This must be our last goodbye, August. It will be better for both of us if you never return.'

Nodding, he took her hands in his. 'Do I still have

your blessing, Sister Joseph?'

'You do, and I will say a prayer for you every night of my life, no matter how long that may be.'

Opening the door they went out onto the stoop. Kansas stood waiting beside the piebald she'd had since Bitterroot Creek. Looking drawn and unhappy, she had tied behind her saddle a small canvas bag containing all her worldly possessions. On seeing Anello she averted her face.

'You are aware that Kansas shot that girl to save you from the guilt of doing so?' Sister Joseph questioned him.

'I know,' he replied hollowly, 'but I am duty bound to report the death and hand Kansas over to the authorities. I will, of course, detail the situation fully.'

'You have a long ride ahead of you, August, which will give you time to ponder on to whom you owe the greatest duty,' Sister Joseph said. 'Now go, and don't look back, not even once.'

Finding it a strain to do so, he obeyed the nun, fighting desperately to form a picture of her in his mind that he might carry forever. Kansas rode a little way behind him, unspeaking. Anello spared neither them nor the horses, riding through the rest of that day and through the night.

They saw the camp up ahead of them in the red light of the next dawn. Anello was relieved to find he had made it just in time. The last of the tents were being pulled down and most of the troopers were mounted, ready to move out. At the head of one formation was Lieutenant George Milnar, who broke

Epitaph of Vengeance 157

the army rules he usually rigidly adhered to, by welcoming Anello with a nod.

As they rode in, Kansas brought the piebald up level with his horse and spoke for the first time since they had left the mission. 'I regret what has happened, August. I had a silly dream in which things were very different between us than they are now. It wasn't to be. I know that you have to do your duty, and swear that it will not change the way I feel about you.'

Finding himself incapable of answering, Anello, aware that, covered in trail dust, he looked nothing like a soldier, headed for where he saw General Meade mounted on a fine white stallion.

'Colonel Anello, so glad you could join us,' the general greeted him in a booming voice that was tinged with sarcasm, yet revealing his pleasure at Anello's return. He turned his deep-sunk eyes to Kansas, who was as unkempt as the worst of saddle tramps, asking, 'And what have we here?'

Looking from the general to the dejected Kansas, and back again, Anello said firmly and clearly, 'This is my lady, General, the woman who is to be my wife.'

'Good for you, Colonel, you took my advice,' Meade said, sweeping his hat off to bow his head to Kansas. 'Be so good as to wait here with the other women, madam, and I will bring your bridegroom back to you safe and sound.'

Orders were shouted then. A few musicians struck up the swinging tune 'Yankee Doodle Dandy' as the army began to move out.

Turning in his saddle, Anello saw Kansas smiling at him. He waved a hand and she waved back. Then he faced the front and headed off for battle.